AURORA'S 1

Club of Dominance 3

Becca Van

MENAGE EVERLASTING

Siren Publishing, Inc.
www.SirenPublishing.com

A SIREN PUBLISHING BOOK
IMPRINT: Ménage Everlasting

AURORA'S DOMS
Copyright © 2013 by Becca Van

ISBN: 978-1-62740-212-5

First Printing: June 2013

Cover design by Harris Channing
All art and logo copyright © 2013 by Siren Publishing, Inc.

Printed in the U.S.A.

PUBLISHER
Siren Publishing, Inc.
www.SirenPublishing.com

DEDICATION

I would like to dedicate this book to my mum. Even when you first found out you were ill with brain cancer you were the strength in the centre of our family. You have fought for nearly thirty years and even though the battle is not over you still stand strong. I admire your courage and tenacity like no other. You are my role model and my heroine. We will stand by your side till the very end.

I love you, Mum. XXOO

AURORA'S DOMS

Club of Dominance 3

BECCA VAN
Copyright © 2013

Chapter One

Aurora Atherton glanced toward the entrance doors to the Club of Dominance as they burst open. She had been greeting guests and members for the last hour and smiled in anticipation of welcoming more people.

The smile faded from her face when she saw the man who had come to the club a few weeks ago with the small, auburn-haired woman—who had ended up collapsing right in front of her. Master Tank had jumped the counter and saved her from hitting the floor, and Masters Turner and Barry had kicked the asshole out and told him he wasn't ever welcome in their club. His face was red, and rage filled his eyes. Aurora stepped away from the counter as he stormed toward her. She cursed her instinctive backward motion because now she couldn't reach the alarm button which was hidden beneath the counter. He pinned her with his eyes and walked around the end of the counter, heading straight for her. She was trapped with no avenue of escape. He was blocking her only exit, and it didn't appear like he was in a reasonable frame of mind. *An understatement if ever there was one, girl.*

Before she could even open her mouth to shout, he had a hard hand wrapped around her throat. The asshole wasn't as big as some of the Doms in the club, but he was stronger than he looked. He lifted her from her feet and shook her. She tried to gasp in air, but her airway was cut off.

"Where the fuck is she, you little slut?" Andrew Mitchell screamed his question into her face, spittle hitting her cheek.

Aurora's head snapped back as he shook her again. Black spots formed before her eyes, and she was in danger of passing out from lack of oxygen.

Fight, Aurora.

She raised her hands, dug her nails into his arm as hard as she could, and dragged them like claws through his flesh. He dropped her like a sack of spuds, her legs buckling as her feet connected with the floor. She yelped when pain shot up her spine as her coccyx hit the unforgiving marble floor. Agony exploded in her cheek, eye, and head when a hard fist hit her face, causing her to moan with pain. *Fuck! That hurt and I didn't even see it coming.* Then she heard footsteps running away and the door slamming closed. What sounded like a motorcycle revved just outside, and then tires screeched and the motor faded into the distance.

Another door crashed, but this time it sounded like it hit the wall and bounced off as it was shoved open, and then heavy footsteps came running toward her. Aurora covered her head and whimpered. There was no way she was letting that bastard get another free shot to her face. Warm hands gripped her upper arms, and she kicked out with her feet and yelled as loudly as she could, hoping that someone inside the club would hear her cries for help and come to the rescue.

"Aurora! Stop fighting me, honey. You're safe."

Aurora stilled as the familiar voice penetrated her adrenaline-laced fear. She looked up into piercing light blue eyes and began to shake. Master Mike lifted her up into his arms and carried her toward the club's internal doors. She turned her face into his chest when she saw Masters Mac, Turner, and Barry watching her with concern.

"I'll man the desk until you can get one of the monitors out here," Master Barry said.

"Garth and Derrick can take over tonight. We have more than enough trained Doms inside to keep an eye on the scenes being played out," Master Turner said.

The noises in the club were a distant din as Master Mike carried her through the great room. Aurora was shaking like a leaf and she was cold to the core. She didn't think she'd ever feel warm again. A high-pitched beep sounded, and then another door slammed closed. She flinched and clutched Master Mike's soft T-shirt. Her throat hurt and her eye and cheek were throbbing painfully, but all she wanted to do was get in a shower and wash that asshole's touch from her body and warm up again. When Master Mike stopped moving she realized that she was sitting on his lap. His thighs felt like steel beneath her legs and ass, and his clean, masculine, spicy scent assailed her nostrils. God, he smelled good.

She had been pining after Master Mike and his brother Master Mac since she had started working at Club of Dominance twelve months ago. This was the first time he had ever touched her and by God did her body sit up and take notice. Aurora had thought the desire for the two men she felt whenever she saw them was strong, but now that one of the masterful Doms was actually holding her, touching her, she realized that had been an understatement. Her areolae contracted and her nipples hardened into tight little peaks and her breasts felt swollen and achy. Her clit throbbed and her pussy clenched and she hoped like hell that he couldn't smell her desire. She was just grateful that she had donned panties, but they were decidedly uncomfortable as they were thoroughly soaked.

She inhaled deeply and groaned when pain shot through her larynx. She shivered and clutched at the warm arms wrapped around her. Finally the shakes slowed and stopped and she was able to take a deep, steadying breath. Large hands shifted her, and then gentle fingers nudged her face up. Her gaze met pools of light blue, and she cringed when she saw the anger in their depths.

"Don't flinch from me, honey. I'm not angry at you, Aurora. I'm angry that you got hurt." Master Mike looked over the top of her head. "Mac, get me some ice. That fucker hit her and she's already swelling and starting to bruise."

A comforting hand ran up and down her back over her corset, and then his flesh rubbed her bare shoulder. Goose bumps broke out on her skin, and she shivered as her body responded to his heat. She wanted to push her skin into his, beg him to touch her all over, but she had never once picked up any vibes from him or Master Mac to let her know that they were interested in her that way. The concern she saw on his face warmed her heart and gave her a little hope. Another gush of cream leaked from her needy pussy.

"Where else are you hurt, honey?"

"My throat," she croaked.

Master Mike tipped her chin up and studied her neck. He growled with fury as he looked at her skin. "Did that fucking asshole try to choke you?"

Master Mac came over and studied her face and neck before he gently placed the towel-wrapped ice pack to her cheek and eye. "I'm going to kill that fucking asshole if I ever lay eyes on him again."

Aurora flinched and gasped as the ice touched her throbbing face. She really would have liked to ask for another ice pack for her neck, but the two Doms already looked angry enough to commit murder and she didn't want to make them any angrier.

"Aurora." Master Turner entered the room with a strange man at his heels. She could tell by his body language and his aura of confidence that he was also a Dom. "This is Dr. Nathan Charleston. He's a good friend of mine and has just set up a new practice on the outskirts of Tigard. I'd like you to let him examine your injuries."

"I'm fine. I don't need a doctor," she rasped out painfully.

Master Turner gave her a hard stare and opened his mouth, but before he could talk Master Mike's firm, cold voice drew her attention. "You most certainly do need to be examined. Do as you're told, sub."

Aurora had heard that Master Mike was a hard man to please and that his eyes turned ice cold when giving orders, but she'd never seen it happen since they hadn't interacted much in the past. The other subs were right, though. She'd never seen such glacial eyes before.

Master Mac squatted down in front of her. He was nearly an exact copy of his brother, but his eyes were a warm, deep blue and his hair was shoulder length where Master Mike's was cut short.

"You need to let the doctor check you over, baby. That asshole could have fractured your cheekbone."

The two brothers were so different yet so similar. Master Mike gave orders and expected them to be obeyed immediately, whereas Master Mac tried to reason and cajole. They seemed to complement each other's personalities, sort of like good cop, bad cop, but Aurora wasn't blind. She'd seen them in action as they took a sub through their paces. They were such hard-assed, arrogant Doms, and she knew Master Mac could be just as harsh as his brother.

Dr. Charleston moved closer and held out his hand. Aurora shook it and let go again. He nudged Master Mac aside and then squatted down next to her.

"You may call me Master Nate. Let me look at your face, sweetheart." Master Nate spoke gently but she was left in no doubt that he would have his way. She sighed and removed the ice pack from her face. Dr. Charleston winced when he saw the damage. He examined her with gentle fingers, but she still ended up flinching when he touched her bruises and swelling. "You're going to have a black eye, sweetie, and your neck is already bruised. Did you get hurt anywhere else?"

Aurora tried to keep her face blank but heat suffused it as she wiggled on Master Mike's lap. Her ass was sore from where she had landed on the floor when that asshole had dropped her.

"I'll take that as a yes." Dr. Charleston was watching her intently. Any other time she would love the way a Dom was able to pick up every nuance of body language, but today she didn't feel like baring her ass to the world.

"Stand up, sub," Master Mike said in a firm voice.

Although Aurora didn't really want to obey him, but she found herself rising to her feet. She lowered her head and kept her eyes on the floor, because if she looked at him he would see the fire in her eyes.

"Strip."

Aurora hesitated as her shaky hands reached for the top clasp on her corset. She didn't feel comfortable being naked in his or Master Mac's presence. As soon as they saw her naked body and how she reacted to their proximity, they would know she was attracted to them. In the whole year she had been working in Club of Dominance, they had never really seen her. Now that they were looking at her for the first time, she felt unsure and vulnerable. The last thing she needed was to see these two men looking at her with pity because her heart was burning for them. Firm hands landed on her shoulders and squeezed slightly. She looked up to see that Master Mac was standing behind her. His eyes were just as icy as his brother's had been, but his warm, gentle touch belied the coldness in his deep blue gaze.

"You were given an order, Aurora. If you don't start doing as you're told you are going to rack up the punishments. Don't think that because you're hurt you won't end up bent over my knee for the spanking you deserve after you've healed. The longer you wait, the more time I'll spend on that delectable little ass."

Aurora turned back to the front and undid her corset. By the time she dropped it on the floor, her hands were shaking. Her breasts felt swollen and needy and her nipples were hard and aching.

She inhaled deeply as she reached the zipper on her skirt, squeezing her legs together as she tried to relieve her throbbing clit. Thank God she had worn panties tonight. Otherwise her inner thighs would already be soaked with her juices. Her pussy clenched and released more cream onto the fabric of her undies. She tried to calm her wayward libido as she pushed her skirt over her hips, which fell to the floor to pool around her ankles and feet. All the while she had been undressing, she was aware of Master Mike's and Master Mac's eyes burning a hole in her body. Everywhere their eyes touched, her skin tingled. When she looked over her shoulder she saw that Master Mike's eyes were glued to her ass.

"Why don't you go and lie down on the bed, Aurora?" Master Nate spoke up.

She was thankful because his voice seemed to cut through the tension surrounding her. The silence in the room was unnerving, but Aurora tried to ignore it as best she could as she walked over to the bed. She climbed up onto the mattress and lay down on her stomach.

"Why don't you tell me where you're hurting, sweetheart?" Master Nate sat on the side of the bed.

"My ass," Aurora said in a near whisper.

Master Nate leaned forward. "I didn't quite hear you, Aurora. Could you repeat that a little louder please?"

Aurora lifted her head from the pillow and glared at Master Nate. From the twinkle in his eye, he had damn well heard what she'd said. But as she watched the gleam left his green eyes and he stared at her expectantly.

Fucking asshole.

"I said my ass," Aurora snapped in a loud voice.

"Okay," Master Nate said, and this time he smiled at her. "I'll have to pull your panties down to take a look."

Aurora tensed as he reached for her hips, but his hands halted in midair when a hard voice stopped him.

"Wait!" Master Mike snapped. "I'll do it."

Aurora thumped her head down onto the pillow and turned to hide her face in its softness. The last thing she needed was Master Mike touching her body. She was having a damn hard time hiding her body's reaction from him and his brother as it was, let alone if they started touching her.

Warm, slightly callused fingers caressed the skin near her hips, and then she heard material tear. Her breathing hitched in her throat and she once again lifted her head and glared over her shoulder. Master Mike's gaze connected with hers and he gave her a hard glower.

"What the hell did you do that for?" Aurora knew as soon as she'd finished speaking she was in trouble. The scowl on Master Mike's face turned to a mask of granite and his eyes iced over. *Oh fuck!*

"Are subs supposed to talk to Doms the way you just did me? That's two."

"What? You can't…"

"Enough!" Master Nate snapped. "You can finish this after I've examined my patient."

Aurora flopped back down onto the pillow and whimpered as her throbbing face hit the material. She also had a hell of a headache. Gloved hands pushed against the top of her ass crack and slowly but gently worked their way down to the end of her coccyx. She flinched when he hit a very tender spot.

"Okay. You have a bruised coccyx bone but it's not broken. You may have trouble sitting for long periods of time so make sure you stand or walk around regularly until the pain subsides."

"Thank you, but I told you I was fine." Aurora went to get off the bed, but Master Nate placed a hand between her shoulder blades and pushed her back down.

"You need to ice your ass, sweetheart. I'll leave you in the hands of these two capable Doms. I'm meeting someone out in the club and I don't want to be late." Master Nate rose to his feet and headed for the door. Just before he left he looked over to Master Mac. "Don't hesitate to call me if you need to."

Master Mac nodded his thanks and then shook Master Nate's hand before closing the door. Aurora once more buried her face in the pillow but this time with more care so she wouldn't hurt her face.

"It's not that bad." Aurora huffed and once more tried to move.

"Don't you dare get off that bed," Master Mac said in a hard voice. Then she heard muffled footsteps and knew he was coming closer. "You will do as the doctor tells you. Turner, have you got any more ice?"

"Yeah, just a sec," Master Turner replied and opened the door, then shouted for his wife. "Charlie, can you get another ice pack, baby?"

Aurora didn't want to be fussed over. All she wanted was to go home, shower, and crawl into bed, but it would be futile to argue with so many Doms. The headache was really beginning to pound, and from previous experience she knew the only thing that would get rid of it was sleep. If she didn't, it would only get worse, and then she would be in real trouble. There was no way she could drive home if she couldn't see properly.

"Are you all right, Aurora?" Charlie asked as she entered the room and brought the ice pack over.

Aurora squinted when she lifted her head from the pillow. "Yes, I'm fine. Thanks, Charlie."

"Okay. Just yell if you need anything."

"Thank you."

Aurora flinched when the ice pack landed on her ass but then settled back down to wait. The more acquiescent she appeared, the sooner everyone would leave her alone. Then maybe she could go home and sleep.

Chapter Two

Mike felt sick to his stomach seeing the bruises already forming on Aurora's face and neck. He wanted to hunt down Andrew Mitchell and beat the shit out of him. He hated to see the pint-sized sub in so much pain. Even though she was a brave little thing and tried to hide it, he could tell she was hurting more than she let on. Mac looked just as angry as he felt, and he knew they were both in trouble.

He had kept his distance from Aurora because he knew she was too good for the likes of him. She was such a sweet, slight thing, almost elfin in appearance, but she was always quick with a smile and she seemed to make friends very easily. His self-imposed rule of never touching a small woman had been really hard to adhere to, but the fear he had of hurting someone so small had helped him to stay away from her. It had been one of the hardest things he'd ever had to do.

Mike thought back to the day he'd first seen her. She had greeted him and Mac with a sunny smile, and although he'd barely glanced her way, the sight of her had been like a punch to the gut.

There she'd been standing behind the reception counter with Master Tank all decked out in her sub wear of a short, hot-pink miniskirt and a black bustier. Her long, wavy blonde hair had been like a halo draped over her shoulders and flowing down her back. Her green eyes sparkled from her pixie-like features, framed in a white-blonde crown of glorious tresses. It had taken everything in him, all the control he had, not to give away the effect she had on him. If he hadn't been such a hard, arrogant bastard, he would have been down on his knees worshipping at her feet. When he glanced toward Mac he'd seen the same punch-drunk shock in his brother's eyes.

Now seeing her beautiful, delicate face all battered and bruised cut him to the quick, and he wanted to scoop her up off that bed and cradle her in his arms, but not just to offer her comfort. He glanced at Mac and saw the same ire and concern on his brother's face at seeing her that way.

Mike hated the way she had her face buried in the pillow as if she was trying to hide from them. His muscles were pumped up with blood and adrenaline, and he wanted to put his fist through a wall, or maybe Mitchell's face. Yeah, that would be better. He looked at Turner as he placed a hand on his shoulder.

"Control that anger, my friend. You don't want to scare her away."

Mike glanced at Aurora, thankful she hadn't heard Turner's whispered statement. Inside he cringed because he thought no one had known how he felt about the little sub. He should have known better. All Doms were trained to watch for body language and to see what wouldn't normally be seen. He spun away from his friend.

"When are you going to put yourself out of your misery?" Turner asked in a low voice.

"Fuck! You don't know what you're asking," Mike whispered through clenched teeth.

"You think I don't? Do you really think you are going to be able to handle seeing her with another Dom? Don't think that she will be single forever. She's had more offers to scene from Doms in this club than any other sub I know."

"She hasn't taken them up on their offers. I've only seen her scene with two Doms the whole time she's worked here."

"Yes, and why do you think that is?"

"How the fuck should I know?"

"Oh, so you have tunnel vision?"

"Why don't you just give it to me straight instead of all the innuendos?"

"Aurora is as innocent as the day she was born. That in itself is appealing to a Dom, but you, my friend, need to open your eyes. I'm going to give her to Garth and Derrick to do a scene with next weekend and you and Mac are going to be the monitors. Instead of trying to ignore her, use your fucking skills and see how much she enjoys being a sub."

Mike didn't get to respond because Turner walked out of the room. Mac stood a couple of feet away, but from the look on his face he hadn't heard a word of their whispered conversation. His brother would have steam coming out his ears if he had. Now they were alone with the woman they had spent the last twelve months trying to avoid.

He looked over at the bed. She looked so fucking small and helpless. Aurora was only an itty bit of a woman. The top of her head didn't reach his shoulders even when she was wearing her fuck-me shoes. She would be lucky to top five two in her bare feet. Her sexy body looked so damn petite and fragile. He was scared to even touch her with his large, paw-like hands, let alone fuck her. Mike was six foot five and built like a brick shithouse. The thought of putting his hands on her and accidentally hurting her with his strength scared the shit out of him. That was why he and Mac always went for taller women who had plenty of padding on their bodies. He didn't have to worry about being too rough or hurting them.

He'd cursed his dominant proclivities from the day he had realized his kink. Being such a big, muscular man and wanting to control women just so he could get off wasn't something he'd ever expected. But when he and Mac had talked about their need to dominate, they had made damn sure to steer clear of any woman they could hurt.

Now, seeing Aurora in such pain, he vowed that he would never scene with her, but the thought of her being with Garth and Derrick and getting off was nearly more than he could stand. His guts churned and his chest ached at having to watch what Turner was setting up.

A slight whimper drew him from his introspection. He walked over to the bed and sat on the edge just as Mac did the same on the other side. Mike brushed Aurora's hair away from her face, being careful not to touch her bruises. Her face was so damn pale, making the marks on her face stand out in stark contrast. She moaned as if she was in pain, and her brow furrowed. When he stroked her head her eyelids lifted.

"Oh God." Her voice was more husky than normal. She was obviously having trouble with her throat after that fucker had tried to crush it. "What are you still doing here?"

"We wanted to make sure you were okay."

"I'm fine. You can leave."

"I don't think so," Mac said firmly.

"Please? Just go so I can sleep."

Mike frowned. She had sounded almost desperate. He let his Dom out and looked at her closely. Aurora frowned and her eyes were glazed over as if she were in a great deal of pain. Her mouth pulled tight, and small white lines deepened around her lips. Perspiration graced her upper lip and forehead. She wasn't fine at all.

All of a sudden she pushed up to her hands and knees and tried to push him aside. He moved, unsure what was going on. She stumbled from the bed and rushed into the adjoining bathroom, slamming the door behind her. He heard her retching through the door.

"Shit. Get Nate back here," Mike ordered and hurried to the bathroom.

Mike crouched behind her, gathered her hair into his hand, and held her forehead while she emptied her stomach. He'd felt her stiffen the moment he touched her, and she would probably have been cursing up a blue streak if she had been able to, but he wasn't about to leave her when she was sick. Her whole body shook and shuddered as she heaved until finally there was nothing left to come up. When he was sure she was done, he flushed the toilet and helped her to her feet. Aurora swayed a little and clutched her head. He picked her up and placed her on the countertop. A little squeal escaped her mouth when her bare ass connected with the cold granite. Then he remembered her sore ass.

"Shit, baby, are you okay? Did I hurt your ass?"

"No, you didn't hurt me, but this counter is damn cold on my naked skin."

He nearly smiled at her answer, relieved that he hadn't hurt her after all, but managed to hide his amusement now that his worry was over. The last thing she needed right at that moment was to see him smirking and to think he didn't care about her welfare.

After rummaging around under the sink he found a clean cloth, a toothbrush still in its packaging, and some toothpaste. He wet the cloth with warm water, wrung it out, and gently washed her face, being careful of her bruising. She sighed and leaned into his hand. Then he opened the toothbrush and placed some paste on the bristles.

"Here you go. Brush your teeth, baby."

Once she was done he carefully lifted her and put her back in bed. Just as he and Mac pulled the covers up, Nate walked in.

"What's the problem?"

"She's sick."

Nate moved to the bed and sat down. "Aurora, what's wrong, sweetheart?"

Mike tensed at the endearment from Nate. He glared at the other man and clenched his fists. He wanted to knock his teeth down his throat and warn him away from his woman.

"Migraine."

"Okay, let me give you a shot of painkillers." Nate reached into his bag and pulled out a syringe and a vial of medicine. "Are you allergic to anything?"

"No."

"Do you get migraines often?"

"Not really." Aurora winced when Nate gave her the shot. "Just when I get too stressed."

"Well, considering what you've been through in the last hour, it's understandable that you'd be stressed right now. The medicine should start working in a couple of minutes. I want you to rest and try and sleep. And don't even think about getting in your car and driving home."

"Thank you, Master Nate." Aurora's eyes drifted closed and she was already slurring her words, but Mike was worried. He had seen the gleam in her eyes when Nate had told her not to drive. She was an independent little thing and he wouldn't put it past her to sleep for a bit and then drive home. There was no way in hell she was doing that. Not on his watch.

Nate must have seen that bit of fire, too. He nodded his head toward the door and then went out into the hallway. "One of you needs to stay with her. She's going to try and leave as soon as she feels capable enough."

"We'll keep an eye on her."

Nate looked from him to Mac and back again and then grinned. "You know, if you two didn't have a previous claim on her you would have a fight on your hands."

"We don't have any claim on her," Mike snapped.

"You don't? Hmm, then maybe things are looking up for Nixon and I after all," Nate said in an even voice.

Mac moved in close to Nate, until the toes of their boots were touching. He gripped the man's T-shirt in a fist. "Don't you dare fucking touch her."

Nate held a hand up palm out and smiled wide. When Mac released him and stepped back, he said, "I'll leave you to take care of *your* woman. Don't hesitate to send for me if you need to." With that Nate walked down the hall and out into the great room, closing the door behind him.

"How the hell does everyone know we want her?" Mac bit out with a scowl on his face.

Mike stared at him without bothering to answer, knowing his brother wouldn't take long to figure things out. The wait was shorter than he thought.

"Fucking Dominant bastards! Do you think she has any idea?"

"Not a clue."

"Turner was right, you know." Mac scrubbed a hand over his face, sighed, and looked through the open door to the bed on the far side of the room. "If we don't claim her someone else will."

"What are you saying?" Mike asked even though he already knew the answer. Mac obviously thought his question was rhetorical. "So let me get this straight. After nearly twelve fucking months of avoiding her, you want to finally make a move?"

"Yep." Mac held his stare and Mike could see the determination in his eyes. And once his brother made up his mind, there was no way he would be swayed from the course he was set on, regardless of the consequences.

Mike lifted his hands and looked down at them. They were just so fucking big. What if he hurt her without meaning to?

Mac gripped his shoulder. "Look at me, damn it."

Mike met Mac's eyes.

"I know that Karen said we hurt her and she was crying, but she was the one who wanted us to dominate her. It was her idea in the first place. If we had known then what we do now we would never have even tried to play with her. What we did had nothing to do with how small she was. That little girl had some serious issues and wanted to be the center of your attention, even to the detriment of her own health. I've already told you God knows how many times that it wasn't just our fault, but hers as well. We stopped as soon as she started crying and yelled stop and then untied her and tried to help her.

"If either of us had known she wasn't into any type of pain we would never have done a scene with her. We were still learning about being Doms and were bound to make mistakes. You weren't the only one to blame for Karen's tears, Mike. She was just as responsible as we were. You have no idea how much I wish we could go back in time and refuse her but she was so insistent that she could take whatever we dished out.

"Fuck, Mike, you didn't even spank her that hard. Yes, her ass was red, but you didn't leave your handprints in her skin. I was probably harder on her than you were. There wasn't a submissive bone in that woman's body. The only reason she wanted to try was because she had the hots for you. I think her tears were more shock than to do with the spanking we gave her. I think she felt defeated because she knew she wouldn't be able to hold your interest if she couldn't play with us. We are fully trained Doms now, damn it. We have learned to read a sub and watch out for every signal a sub gives off.

"Dominating a sub has nothing to do with their size. You have dominated other women here and never had a complaint and not once have any of those subs used their safe word. Just because a woman is taller or has a little more padding doesn't mean that their pain is any less than someone smaller. You of all people should know that everyone's pain threshold is different. When are you going to start trusting yourself, Mike?

"When are you going to start believing me? Shit." Mac threw his hands in the air. "I give up. You just go on the way you are, but I'm not going to stand by and watch some other fucking Dom claim our woman. She's ours and there is no way in hell I'm letting her slip through our fingers. I'm done, Mike. I'm done waiting for you to get your head out of your ass and open your eyes to see what's right in front of your face. You're either in or you're out, but either way Aurora is going to be my sub."

Mike watched as his brother sat in a chair beside the bed and sighed. He couldn't imagine having to see Aurora every day and not being able to touch her, hold her, and love her now that he'd had her in his arms and inhaled her sweet scent. It would be pure torture. Never in his life had he felt so torn. His heart ached and he rubbed between his pecs, trying to relieve the pain.

What am I going to do? Is Mac right? Had he taken too much onto his own shoulders where Karen was concerned? Was she equally to blame for her tears? Had her tears been because she realized that she would never really be able to connect with him? Because she had discovered she wasn't submissive and into erotic pain after all? He tried to remember what had gone down that day.

* * * *

Mike had never felt such a rush in his life. Karen was trussed up in the basement where he and Mac had set up their gym equipment. There she was on the weight bench with her arms and legs cuffed and restrained, her naked body displayed for their pleasure. His muscles were pumped and adrenaline fired through his system.

She was such a little thing and even though she had a slight frame she was curved in all the right places. Her breasts were small and perky, topped with pretty pink nipples which were hard and standing up at attention. He licked his lips as he tried to imagine what those pink little berries would taste like. The hair on her pubis matched the hair on her head, and she was obviously aroused. Light caused the drops of dew clinging to her red pubic hair to glisten. It would have been much better if her pussy had been bare, but that would have to wait for another day. Maybe when she got to know them better she would let them shave her so that her pussy lips would be on display for their carnal delight.

Mike took a step forward and crouched down near her head. He fisted her hair and slammed his mouth down on hers. The little whimpering sounds she made as he kissed her caused his cock to jerk and throb as it pulsed against the zipper of his jeans. God, I can't wait to fuck that tight, wet cunt.

When he finally lifted his head he saw that Mac was already eating out her pussy. She sobbed and tried to arch up into his brother's mouth, but Mike was having none of that. They were in control, not her. He reached over and slapped her thigh. "Don't move, sub."

Karen glared at him and opened her mouth, but she closed it again when he gave her a hard stare. Mac lifted his head and rose to his feet. "You've just earned a punishment, sub. You know better than trying to top from the bottom. We've already told you the rules and you agreed to them. Help me turn her over."

Mike helped Mac remove the cuffs and then between them they turned Karen over and restrained her again. She glared daggers at Mike.

"That's two, Karen."

Mac ran his hand over her bare ass until her muscles relaxed. Then he struck out, raining slaps down on her fleshy globes, alternating to each cheek until he reached the count of ten. When Mike lifted her head to check on her, he held in a smile. Karen's eyes were glazed with fury. He wanted to tap into that passion and couldn't wait to earn her submission.

"It's your turn to punish our little sub, Mike."

Mike looked at her red ass and smoothed his hands over her butt cheeks. Karen wiggled and sighed, but he could tell the sigh was one of contented arousal. He and Mac had been taking Dom classes at the Club of Dominance from Masters Turner and Barry, and they had learned to read body language and all the signs a sub emitted. It was important to watch their sub for fear or pain. The last thing a Dom wanted to do was hurt their sub, but since her ass was already quite pink, Mike decided to go easy on her. He started off slow and gave a tap to each cheek. Then with each swat he added more power, but he never once put his all into those slaps. He and Mac were both big men and he never wanted to cause any real pain to a woman. By the time he counted ten, his palm was tingling pleasantly and the skin on Karen's butt was healthy ruddy color.

"Stop. I can't take any more."

Just as he reached for the cuff around her ankle he heard a sniffle. He glanced at Mac and then they both hurried to release her and he tried to pick her up. She smacked him in the chest and then started yelling at him.

"Don't touch me. God, you are such a brute. I can't believe you hurt me like that."

"What..."

Karen moved toward her clothes and with jerky movements put them on. She kept her face turned away from him as if she couldn't bear to look at him. Mike stared at his hands and then clenched his fists. He didn't think he'd hurt her. He'd been more lenient on her than Mac had, or he thought he had. Maybe he was stronger than he thought. What the fuck?

"Karen, talk to me, honey. What's going on?" Mac asked.

Karen had glanced toward him and all he could see were the tears streaming down her face. God, did I hurt her that much? *"You two are sick. I never want to see either of you again."*

Her voice drifted away as Mac followed her up the stairs. Mike sank down on the bench and vowed then and there that he would never touch another small woman again. Obviously he couldn't trust himself not to screw up and hurt someone of her size. He was a Dominant, but to be able to tend to his own needs he would have to make sure he played with women who had more padding. Waifs were definitely out.

Mac came back down the stairs. "Don't you believe what she said, Mike. You didn't hurt her. I spanked her a lot harder than you did and she didn't complain. That woman has been hankering for you for weeks. She probably thought that she could play at being submissive without any problem but she isn't a sub, Mike."

"Or maybe I'm stronger than we think."

"Bullshit. God, how could you not have seen through that act? She was hoping to be able to be what you needed, but she can't. Karen is too dominant herself. Maybe she had a problem with the whole ménage thing, but you didn't fucking hurt her. She was aroused by the thought of having sex but not the discipline. Jesus, I want to get her back here and show her what real discipline is all about. She was manipulating you, hoping she could snag you, but there was no way in hell she was ever going to submit and you fell for it."

Mike didn't want to listen to any more. He strode across the room, up the stairs, snagged a beer from the fridge in the kitchen, and kept walking until he was ensconced in his room.

* * * *

Mike straightened from his lounging position on the wall and walked back into the bedroom. He sat in the chair across from Mac as he watched Aurora sleep.

"You were right. Karen wasn't a sub and I didn't hurt her that much. She just wasn't into pain," he said in a low voice so he wouldn't disturb Aurora with his voice.

"So are you in?" Mac asked.

"Yeah, I'm in."

Chapter Three

Aurora moaned as she stretched. Her body still ached, her cheek and eye throbbed, and she felt a little seedy from the lasting effects of her migraine and the pain medication, but she felt much better since she'd been able to sleep. She rolled over onto her back and blinked a few times to clear her vision. A rustle to the side caused her to turn her head toward the sound. Master Mike was sitting in an armchair staring at her. As she looked into his eyes she watched as they turned from ice cold to blazing hot within the blink of an eye.

Is he that mad at me? God, what have I done to deserve his anger?

Another sound like a shuffle from the other side of the bed drew her attention. She looked up into hungry eyes as her gaze met Master Mac's.

She closed her eyes and tried to pretend they weren't there. Of course, that was entirely impossible. As soon as her eyes had landed on them her body had started to respond. *Shit! What are they still doing here?*

"How are you feeling, sweet thing?"

Aurora shivered as Master Mac's deep cadence washed over her. Would she ever get used to such a deep, gravelly voice?

"I'm good."

"Look at me when you talk to me, sub," Master Mac demanded.

Oh, no way, no how. Does he think he is going to control me just because he is a badass Dom? Not in this fucking lifetime. Especially after the way he and his sanctimonious brother have ignored me for nearly a whole year. And as far as she was concerned she wasn't working or playing, so they were just men at the moment, not Masters.

"I gave you an order, Aurora. I expect to be obeyed."

"Piss off!" There was no way in hell she was letting someone who didn't care about her tell her what to do. She thought back over her lonely life and wondered if she would ever find what she was looking for.

Aurora had realized from approximately the age of sixteen that she was different from the other girls at school. She had watched as they had all flirted with the opposite sex and went out on dates, but for some reason those boys had done nothing for her. The thought of having a single boyfriend left her feeling cold, but that wasn't the only reason and she hadn't a clue as to why she didn't want to mix with the boys of her peerage. It wasn't that she hadn't had anyone ask her out. She had been asked out, a lot, at first, but she'd never felt a spark, so she had continued to decline until she'd earned a reputation of being frigid. Even though that label had hurt in the beginning she'd done a lot of soul searching and knew that it wasn't true. At least she didn't think it was.

She yearned to be loved just like any other female, and although she had spent some lonely years as she went through high school and most of college being single and without any true girlfriends, she had decided she was going to hold out for her true loves. Yes, loves. Aurora knew she wouldn't be satisfied with just one man.

She'd found all the answers she'd been looking for by chance. Aurora had been walking through downtown Tigard in Northern Oregon after she'd finished college for the day and had seen a display of books in a shop window. The picture on the cover had called to her and she found herself inside the store reading the blurb on the back cover before she could blink. It was about a ménage relationship but also about BDSM. She'd bought the book there and then and hurried back to her one-bedroom efficiency. She had spent the next few hours reading about the trials and tribulations the heroine went through as she struggled to come to terms with being in a relationship with two Dominant men and what it meant to be a submissive.

She'd laughed and cried along with the heroine, but as she'd read the BDSM and sex scenes her body had begun to ache and her panties had become wet for the first time in her life. Aurora had masturbated for the first time ever as she imagined those two Doms playing with her in a BDSM club and then making her come over and over again. By the time she'd finished reading the story she'd known that she wanted what the heroine in the story had. She wanted to be a permanent sub with two Masters who loved her more than any other woman.

Aurora was a submissive and proud of it, and she wasn't about to settle for anything less than her body and heart's desire. When she'd seen the advertisement for the position of reception duty for the Club of Dominance, just as she'd finished her business management degree, she had jumped in with both feet and she hadn't looked back.

She'd dabbled a little with a couple of Doms, but she should have held out. It had been a mistake she couldn't take back. She'd been so full of expectations, but she'd known in the first five minutes of the scene that her heart wasn't in it. The two Doms had been frustrated because she'd shown no arousal at all and had called a halt to the session. There hadn't been a connection with those men at all and she had just gone through the motions until they'd stopped the play.

She was glad she'd placed a hard limit of no sex on her paperwork when she'd filled it out, but what Dom would want a twenty-four-year-old virgin? She'd been spanked, whipped with a flogger, had candle and cup play, but not once had she ever experienced subspace or climaxed.

Aurora had begun to think that she really was frigid, that maybe all those boys in school and college had been right, but then she saw Master Mike Tanner with his short sandy-colored hair and beautiful blue eyes, and her body had responded immediately. Master Mike was masculinity personified, and he got her libido revving without even looking at her. He was a very tall, muscular, handsome man, any sub's wet dream, and his brother, Master Mackenzie "Mac" Tanner, was just as sexy. They were so similar in looks she thought they had to be twins. The only differences she could see were that Master Mike was about an inch taller than Master Mac, and their hair was different lengths, and the color of their eyes differed by the depth of their blue irises.

But it was like she didn't even exist. Neither man had ever seemed to "see" her at all. She had been invisible to them until now, and she couldn't work out what had changed to make them actually see her for the first time. She gave a wistful sigh and pushed her longing aside as the masculine voice pulled her back to the present.

"Oh, you are just begging for a spanking, sub," Master Mike said in a cold voice.

Aurora pushed herself up in bed, taking care to pull the quilt with her so that her nakedness wasn't exposed. She already felt vulnerable and at a disadvantage by being in bed, let alone nude.

"Look, you two arrogant asses. I'm not currently working or playing and you're not my Doms, so I don't have to call you Master. Besides, respect is earned, not demanded."

The fire in their eyes dimmed a little, and Aurora was able to relax as they looked at each other rather than at her. Then Mike surprised her by nodding his head at her. "You're right. I'm sorry. We were worried about you. It is hard for us to see such a petite woman injured."

Aurora had never heard him apologize to anyone before. She figured it had been a hard thing for him to do since he was such a hard-ass Dom, but what struck her most was the fact that he was only concerned for her because of her size, not because they cared for who she was.

They hardly ever look at me, let alone speak to me.

Mac rose from his chair, and she looked up to see his face was set in a granite mask. He threaded his fingers through his hair and sighed.

"We'll leave you to rest. We should have left for home hours ago." He left the room without a backward glance.

Mike stood and stared at her mutely. "Take care of yourself, Aurora." He, too, left without looking back and closed the door behind him.

Aurora sat watching the door, wondering what she had just done. *Have I burned all my bridges? God, I want them so much.* Tears pricked the backs of her eyelids, but she blinked a few times and pushed her sadness aside. Being careful not to disturb all her aches and pains, she got out of bed and headed for the bathroom. Once she'd showered and dressed, she was going home. She glanced at the digital clock on the bedside table as she walked past and saw that it was three in the morning. She'd slept way longer than she normally would have and figured that the painkillers Nate had given her plus the stress of the day had caught up with her. Well, it didn't matter now.

She rubbed her aching chest and stepped into the shower, feeling totally dejected. At least she would get to see Mike and Mac at the club even if they wouldn't have anything to do with her. Aurora didn't think she'd ever be able to be with any other man, or in her case, men. Seeing those two arrogant Doms on a daily basis was going to kill her inside, but at least she would be able to see them if only from afar. What she wouldn't give to have them touching her with their hands and mouths and cocks. She'd only had a small taste of their skin touching hers and feeling the heat from their bodies. She wondered if that would be able to sustain her for the rest of her life.

Not bloody likely.

* * * *

"Fuck!" Mac slammed his hand down on the steering wheel as he drove. "We've fucked up big-time."

"Yeah," Mike sighed.

"Do you think she'll ever want to have anything to do with us again?"

"I don't know, probably not. God, she looked so damned hurt."

"It's no fucking wonder after what we did to her. She looked so damn fragile in that big bed with her face pale except for the bruising and swelling. I can't believe we went all Dom on her after being attacked. How could we have been so stupid?" Mac glanced over to his brother.

"We weren't thinking with our brains. That's for sure."

"Maybe we should just stop going to the club." Mac signaled and then changed lanes. "It's not like we have any interest in playing with any of the subs. Well, anyone but Aurora."

"Yeah, I don't know if I can stand to see her every day and not be able to touch her. Why did it take me so frickin' long to figure out Karen wasn't submissive?"

"Because at the time you weren't ready to see the truth." Mac turned into the drive and stopped the truck. "She got to you when we were just new to the scene. You weren't as confident playing at being a Dom yet. Don't beat yourself up, Mike. As long as you finally figured out she was as much to blame as we were, is all that matters."

"Yeah, I suppose so. God, my cock is so fucking hard right now. I feel like such a bastard for having a boner when she was hurt. Man, I can still feel her in my arms and her sweet ass on my lap."

"Asshole." Mac gave him a grin. "At least one of us was able to hold her. She is so sweet. She smells so damn good I want to lick over every inch of her delectable little body. Are all those rules you made after being with Karen still in play? Are you going to balk if we can finally get Aurora to play with us, or are you going to man up and pull your inner Dom to the forefront and trust yourself to read a sub?"

"Fuck," Mike sighed and scrubbed a hand over his face. "I'm still worried that I could hurt her, Mac, but the thought of her being with anyone but us fills me with rage. There is no fucking way I am about to let some other Dom snap her up before we've even had a chance. I want her just as much as you do."

"She hardly ever plays at the club," Mac said and looked at Mike. "How the hell are we going to gain her trust and get her to play with us?"

"I'm not sure yet, but we have to figure something out and fast."

Mac got out of the truck and unlocked the front door. He stilled and raised his fist, knowing his brother would become alert. The hair on the back of his neck prickled and he glanced around the hallway. The house didn't feel right, as if someone was there and shouldn't be or something was out of place. He went into soldier mode, which was easy since both he and Mike were non-active Marines.

He and his brother had spent eight years serving their country and had been lucky enough to come home safe and sound. Some of their team hadn't been so lucky. It had been really hard dealing with the grief and loss, but knowing that their friends had lost their lives in the Middle East and would never have the chance to marry or see their families grow had really disillusioned him and Mike. There would forever be conflict and terrorism in this world as long as the religious fanatics thought their way was better. Mac had no problem with people having their faith, but when innocent people were killed and tortured because they didn't conform to what others believed it made him sick to his stomach. And the same went with dictators pushing their beliefs onto others because they were greedy for wealth and power. Why couldn't people just get along and live in peace and harmony? Even though he and Mike had been proud to serve their country, once their time was up, neither of them had signed back up.

Once out of the military they had seen a need in their hometown for more removal companies and had pooled their money to start up their own business. It had taken a couple of years but now their company was doing so well, they had quite a large contingency of employees and never had to move another piece of furniture if they didn't want to. Not that he or Mike minded working. They didn't, but it was nice to know they had financial security as well as trusted employees.

They searched the house and found nothing, but he was still unsettled. Something wasn't right.

"Anything?"

"No, but my skin's still crawling," Mike replied.

"Mine, too." Mac entered the kitchen and snagged two beers then passed one over to his brother. "You know, it's easy to blame all the shit that's been going on at the bay on kids, but it makes you wonder now."

"Yeah, maybe so. Worth looking into, anyway. What I'd like to know is how the fucker got in. There are no broken windows or signs that any of them were forced open and the alarm isn't going off."

"Yeah, that doesn't sit well with me. The only other way…" Mac straightened from his slouched position on the counter and headed for the front door. "Check the back and the garage."

Mac pulled the front door open and flicked the entrance and porch lights on. There were a couple of small scratches on the metal surrounding the keyhole. "Someone picked the fucking lock. Whoever it is tried to make damn sure we didn't know they'd been here. Nothing was out of place."

"My gut churned more in the office," Mike said and turned back down the hall. Mac came up behind him as they both stood inside their home office, looking intently around the room.

"Someone was here, all right. I know damn well that pad was next to the phone. It's across the other side of the desk now. You know how I always leave it close to the phone so we can take down any messages."

"What the hell would anyone want with us? We haven't made any nemeses as far as I know. And the only people who know we are retired Marines are the friends we served with."

"Fuck if I know." Mike scrubbed a hand over his face. "There's nothing we can do about it now. Let's get a few hours sleep. Thank

God we don't have to work tomorrow. I'm going to call Garth first thing and see if he can put in a better security system with cameras.

"Shit!" Mike turned to face Mac. "Speaking of Garth…Turner has arranged for Aurora to scene with Garth and Derrick next weekend."

"What?" Mac slammed his fist down on the desk. "Un-fucking-believable. Why would he do that?"

"There's more." Mike hesitated.

"Spit it out," Mac snapped.

"He's appointed us as scene monitors."

"Jesus H. Christ. Why the hell would he do that? Is he trying to torture us?"

Mike sighed. "I think he's trying to make us jealous. Fucking asshole! How the fuck are we going to watch two of our friends play with our sub and not rip their fucking throats out?"

"God only knows." Mac finished off the last of his beer and went to dump the bottle in the recycle bin. Mike was just coming out of the office.

"I think we should just avoid the club altogether. That way we won't see what they do to her and we won't try and kill them for touching our sub."

"Wait!" Mac exclaimed. "Did you see any of the scenes Aurora did?"

"Yeah, fuck it."

"I did, too." Mac held up his hand to cut Mike off. "None of the Doms laid a hand on her."

"What?" Mike straightened with interest.

"The Doms only used a switch and paddle on her. They never touched her with any part of their body."

"Well, thank heavens for small mercies." Mike frowned. "Why didn't I notice that?"

"Knowing you, you were probably too pissed off to notice it."

"Yeah, you're right. I had to walk away after the first minute or I would have started a fight. Why would she do a scene and not let a Dom touch her?"

"Now there's a question I wish I knew the answer to. You know, now that I think back, I don't think Aurora was engaged at all. She looked downright bored."

"The Doms must have been new to play. Any good Dom in their right mind would know how to get a sub off even without laying a hand on her."

"You would think that, wouldn't you?" Mac grinned.

"What aren't you telling me?"

"The Doms weren't new."

"Who were they?"

"Luke and Matt Plant." Mac watched as a slow smile spread across Mike's face. The tension left his brother and he knew they wouldn't be avoiding the club after all.

"Interesting."

"Isn't it, though?" Mac walked toward his bedroom, but before he closed the door he glanced back at Mike. "When Garth and Derrick arrive to outfit the new security system I think maybe we should have a little talk with them."

"That's a definite, not a maybe."

Mac chuckled as he closed his bedroom door. He stripped and got into bed. *Maybe things aren't as bleak as they first seemed.*

* * * *

Mike watched as Derrick did the last check on their new security system. He and his brother Garth Jackson had made sure that Mac's and Mike's cell phones would alert them if anyone broke into the house. Small cameras had been placed around their property, inside and out, which would record any images on a system that was hidden in the back of the hall utility cupboard. Mike was curious and had wanted to begin questioning his friends as soon as he'd seen them get out of their truck, but had held off.

"Do you think you could update our security at the warehouse?" Mike asked Derrick.

"Sure. What do you have?"

"Just an alarm on the doors," Mike replied and then sighed. "We've had a spate of break-ins and vandalism. I thought it was just kids fooling around but after the break-in here I'm not so sure."

Derrick glanced at him and then back to the panel on the wall. "Windows have been smashed and the office was ransacked. Nothing was taken but all the files were rifled through and the papers on our desks were strewn about the place. Graffiti was left all over the walls inside and out plus left on the side of a couple of trucks."

"Sounds like kids."

"That's what I thought, too, but now, I just don't know."

"Do you want the same setup as we're putting in here at the warehouse?"

"Yeah, but make sure that you put cameras all around the outside. That way if anyone manages to break in we'll have them on camera."

"Okay."

"Thanks."

Derrick looked up at him as he closed the panel which would hide the recording device from view. "What else is on your mind?"

"Has Turner contacted you yet?"

"Ah…shit."

"I'll take that as a yes."

Derrick nodded.

"Have you scened with Aurora before?" Mike glanced to the side when he saw Mac walk close and lean against the wall. His brother crossed his arms over his chest in a nonchalant pose, but Mike wasn't fooled. He could see the tension in Mac's muscles and the slight tightness around his mouth.

"No."

"Have you watched her play?"

Derrick nodded.

"Tell me what you saw," Mike demanded.

A frown marred Derrick's face and Mike could tell he was thinking before he spoke.

"I don't want you beating around the bush. Just give it to me straight."

"About six months ago she did a scene with Matt and Luke." Derrick sighed. "I don't understand it, but from what I could see she wasn't into the play at all. Her eyes wandered from them to other scenes and she looked totally bored."

"That must have gone down well," Mike commented, knowing how dominant Luke and Matt were. Not being able to engage a sub in scene play would be a real ego booster. *Not.*

"Yeah, like a fucking hole in the head. They finished up without seeing it through."

"Do you think she's just playing at being a sub but not truly submissive?"

Derrick looked at him as if he had rocks in his head. "What do you think?"

"She's definitely a sub."

Derrick nodded and looked toward Mac. Then their gazes connected again. "They're not the only ones who had trouble engaging her."

"Explain."

"She did a scene with Jack and Tank once. They used wax play and cupping."

"Shit, she didn't stand a chance. Those two are the best I've seen at that play. She would have been in subspace within ten minutes."

Derrick shook his head.

"No?"

"Nope. Same thing. She just lay on that table and stared at the ceiling."

"Shit. What the hell?"

"Turner stepped in and halted play. He took Aurora aside and spoke to her. She looked kind of embarrassed, but by the end of the discussion she looked…resigned."

"Any idea what they talked about?"

"I don't have a clue."

"Thanks, Derrick." Mike stepped back and led the way to the kitchen. "Do you want some coffee?"

"Yeah, thanks."

As Mike made the coffee, Mac and Garth entered the kitchen. They sat around talking for a while, but Mike spaced out from time to time. He wondered why a natural-born submissive would struggle to respond to four well-trained Dominants in two separate scenes.

Now that was a question he would like very much to find out the answer to.

Chapter Four

The club was nearly filled to capacity and Aurora was pretending to have fun, greeting members, laughing and joking with them as they signed in. It was Friday night and even though this was only her third shift of the week, she was exhausted. Ever since that night she had been attacked by that asshole Mitchell and then been watched over by Mike and Mac, she had hardly slept a wink. Mitchell had died in a car accident after abducting Emma from the club, and even though she would never wish death upon anyone, she was relieved that she didn't have to be worried about him coming in and beating on her again. That bastard had done a real number on her but she should be over it by now. He was no longer a threat to anyone, but the nightmares persisted.

Every time she closed her eyes she felt that fucker's hand around her throat cutting off her air supply. When she finally slept it was to dream. The dream was the same each night. It started out with Masters Mike and Mac touching her, kissing her, and playing her body until she was one big aching mass of need begging them to make love with her. Just when she was about to get her wish, the eroticism of the dream changed to a nightmare. Her dream lovers faded away, and in their place was Mitchell with his hands on her body, making her feel so violated and dirty. Why her conscience changed from the loving scene to one of horror when that bastard hadn't touched her in any sexual way, she had no clue. But she didn't know how much more she could stand. She was a mess in more ways than one.

Aurora had actually taken the time to put on makeup for tonight. She had dark smudges beneath her eyes and still had some bruising on her cheek that she was trying to hide, and because she wasn't sleeping, she was so anxious she wasn't eating much either. The thought of food made her feel physically ill, and she only managed a few bites to eat over the last five days. She let the smile fall from her face as the latest members to enter disappeared through the internal double doors to the club, and she lowered herself into the chair with a sigh.

Masters Matt and Luke were taking turns being with her at the reception counter, and Master Luke was currently speaking on the phone. When he shifted she glanced over to see him watching her with a frown. She looked away quickly and cursed the heat suffusing her cheeks. Aurora had attempted a scene with him and his brother, and she hadn't felt a thing when they had played with her. She was deeply embarrassed over that incident and had hoped she wouldn't have to spend much time with them, but it seemed she was being thwarted in all directions lately.

What the hell is wrong with me? Why can't I feel anything when I submit? I know I'm submissive inside, so why can't I let go?

Aurora felt like she would never experience the deep-seated need of true submission and wondered if she was just wasting her time. *Maybe all those boys in high school and college were right. Maybe I am just so fucking cold inside that nobody will ever get through the layers of ice.* The word *frigid* hovered on the edges of her mind.

Master Turner had taken her aside quite a few months back and suggested she not play in the club until she was truly ready. She could remember that conversation like it was yesterday and didn't think she would ever forget it. God, she was so naïve. How the hell had he known how she felt? She had been so careful and tried not to let on to anyone what her feelings were, but it seemed her efforts had been futile. Sometimes she wished she had never discovered the world of BDSM. If she hadn't, maybe she would be in a vanilla relationship and happy enough with her lot, because she wouldn't have known what was missing.

* * * *

"*Aurora, why do you persist trying to scene with Doms you have no connection to?*" *Master Turner asked.*

"*Sorry, Master?*"

Master Turner sighed. "*You, little sub, have a very loving heart. We both know that no matter how hard you try, no one but the men you love will be able to make you react. You aren't ready to play with other Doms, Aurora. I would really appreciate it if you didn't play unless your heart was in it, honey. You are damaging my Doms' egos.*"

Aurora's face flushed. She lowered her eyes and shifted uncomfortably.

"*Will you do something for me?*" *Master Turner asked and waited for her to meet his eyes.*

"*If I can, Master Turner.*"

"*I want you to think about playing out a scene with Masters Mike and Mac.*" *He held up his hand and gave her a stern look when she opened her mouth to interrupt.* "*Don't interrupt me, sub. We both know you want to, Aurora, so please don't you dare insult my integrity by denying it. You are the sort of woman who will love once and deeply. You won't ever be able to endure another's touch. Please, just go and ask them to top you. But if you can't find the courage you need to face the men you care for, don't ask or accept scene plays from other Doms unless you can give them your true submission.*"

Aurora didn't know how to respond to or face such blatant truthfulness. She tried to lower her head, but Master Turner reached out, cupping her chin to stop the action.

"*I'm not trying to hurt you, Aurora, but if you continue on the way you have, you may end up doing more damage than good. How are you going to feel if you finally find a Dom who can reach you physically? I know you, sub. You are going to tear yourself up inside if you give yourself to a man or men you don't love. You will never be able to look yourself in a mirror again. You will feel like you have betrayed your heart and soul. Give them time, honey. They will come around eventually, and the wait will be worth it.*

"Don't ever doubt the passion you have buried deep inside. It's there just waiting for the right men to tap into. You are a true submissive, Aurora, but you need to have your heart engaged to give up that tight control."

Master Turner took hold of her hand. "Now, why don't we go and sit at the bar for a while. We can share a drink, and I want you to relax for a few minutes and think about what I've said."

Master Turner helped her onto a stool and ordered her a drink. She sat and thought over everything he had said and knew he was right. She wasn't in love with Masters Luke and Matt, so she had been locked up tighter than a chastity belt inside. Making the decision then and there to not play in another scene was like a weight lifting from her shoulders. There were only two men she wanted to be with, and no one else would ever do.

* * * *

Aurora came back to the present with a start when Master Luke spoke. "Have you been ill, Aurora?"

"No, Master Luke."

"You've lost weight and your clothes are much looser than they should be. You have dark smudges beneath your eyes and you're pale beneath that makeup. Are you sure you're well?"

"Yes, Master Luke. I'm fine, but thank you for asking."

"At least that bruise on your cheek and eye has nearly gone." Luke picked up a bottle of water and removed the cap. "Here, drink this. You look like you're about to pass out."

Aurora took the bottle gratefully and drank deeply. By the time she lifted it away from her lips half the bottle was gone. "Thanks, Master Luke."

"You aren't sleeping," Master Luke stated, and she just gave a negligible shrug.

What was there to say when someone stated the obvious?

"Are you having nightmares?"

Aurora looked up, startled, and quickly looked away again, mentally cursing the fact that she worked with such highly trained, perceptive, and intuitive Doms. She had thought she had learned to hide her feelings well, but she couldn't seem to hide anything from the Doms who visited the Club of Dominance. *Did they have to take lessons on How to Read Subs 101?*

The interior doors to the club opened and Master Turner walked toward her. Aurora sighed with relief at Master Turner's timing. She had just been saved by the proverbial bell. *Thank God.*

"Master Luke, how are things?"

"The usual for a Friday night, but no incidents."

"Good." Master Turner shifted his attention to her. "I need you inside, Aurora."

A knot formed in her stomach, but she had no idea why. It wasn't like she was in trouble or anything. *Is it?*

Taking a deep breath, she rose to her feet and followed Master Turner into the great room. The sights and sounds which drifted to her ears caused an ache deep inside, only it wasn't a sexual ache. It was one of envy. *God, why can't I have that?* Her eyes drifted to the scene being played out on stage. A female sub was being whipped with a flogger, and from the dreamy expression on her face she was deep into subspace.

Bringing her mind back to the present, she followed Master Turner to the rooms off to the side and stopped behind him when he halted. She looked through the glass and her breath hitched in her throat. Masters Garth and Derrick were preparing the room for a scene, but there was no sub in sight. *Surely Master Turner doesn't want...*

"Aurora, I want you to do a scene with Masters Garth and Derrick."

Her mouth dropped open and she felt her eyes widen in shock. *Why does he want me to play with these two Doms? Wasn't he the one to advise me I shouldn't scene with any of the Masters in the club?*

Master Turner reached out and nudged her chin up. Aurora swallowed, and from the concern on Master's face, he had heard her.

"Do you trust me, Aurora?"

She did trust Master Turner, but she wasn't sure he knew what he was doing right at this moment.

"Yes, Master."

"Excellent. I want you to go in there and give over control to those two Doms."

"But..."

"Don't speak, sub. You don't want to be racking up punishments before you've even started," Master Turner said in a firm voice. "Aurora, I know what I'm doing. Please, just trust me?"

"Okay, Master," she replied and cursed the little squeak in her voice.

"Good girl. Now go on in. Just remember you can use your safe word whenever you like. What is the word you use if you need a break?"

"Yellow, Master."

"Good girl. And what is your safe word to stop proceedings?"

"Red, Master."

"Give me your wrists, Aurora."

She held them up to him and watched as he wrapped the wide, fluffy, lined leather cuffs around them and then snapped them together in front of her.

"Very good," Master Turner praised then gripped her shoulders and turned her toward the door, giving her a gentle shove. "You're safe, honey. Just remember no one will do anything you don't want. Every Dom in this club knows how to read a sub, Aurora. You have nothing to worry about."

That's easy for you to say. You're not the one frozen inside and you won't be the one at the mercy of two Doms.

Aurora stepped over the threshold, her stomach churning with anxiety. She felt as if her life was about to change forever and she had no control over it. But what confused her most was she had no idea why, because she felt nothing for the two Doms waiting for her.

Aurora wondered if Master Turner had seen something in her that indicated she was ready to try play again. She trusted Master Turner like no other. He was such a nice, caring man and hoped he knew what he was doing. Maybe Master Turner thought she could submit to Masters Garth and Derrick when she hadn't been able to submit to any other Dom. *Well, I'm about to find out.*

* * * *

Mac watched Aurora as she walked toward Garth and his brother. She kept her head and eyes lowered like the perfect little sub, but he could see the tension in her muscles. When she lowered herself to the kneeling slave position on the floor then placed her hands on her thighs palms up, he saw the way they trembled.

He wanted to go haring into that room and take over before the scene began but Turner had asked Garth and Derrick to scene with her for some unknown reason he had yet to determine. Then it hit him. Turner was trying to make him and Mike jealous. He should have figured out right away when Mike had told him about setting up this scene. The sneaky bastard was trying to make them make a move on the one woman they had coveted for nearly twelve months.

Aurora looked like she was ready to bolt. When Turner had first asked his friends to play with her earlier that evening, he had heard Derrick adamantly refuse. Mac wondered if Mike had already figured out what Turner was up to and hoped to God his plan didn't backfire. He glanced at Mike standing at his side. His jaw was clenched tight as were his fists and he could see the muscle ticking in his brother's jaw. He hoped like hell Turner knew what the fuck he was doing. The last thing they needed was to cause psychological damage to Aurora before she relented to be with her men. Because Mac had no doubt in his mind that Aurora wouldn't respond to the Doms in that room with her. She hadn't responded to any other Dom so far, so why would Derrick and Garth be any different?

"Very pretty, little sub," Derrick praised. "Stand up now."

Mac was glad that he could hear the other Doms when they spoke to Aurora. If she said her safe word he would be in there faster than the other two could blink. He relaxed his muscles as much as he could and waited to see how the scene would unfold.

Aurora rose to her feet and stood statue still, waiting for their next command. Garth moved close to her back so she could feel the heat of his body and Mac watched for a reaction. There was none.

"Strip, Aurora."

She lifted trembling hands to the bodice of her corset and undid the clasps one by one and then dropped the garment to the floor. He wondered if she was trying to test Garth and Derrick, because all subs knew to fold their clothes and put them on one of the chairs around the edge of the room.

"That's one," Garth stated in a firm voice.

Aurora winced and bent to retrieve the corset and quickly folded it and put it on the nearest chair. Maybe she hadn't dropped it on purpose after all. The trembling in her hands had spread and now her arms were also shaking slightly. *You'd better know what you're fucking doing, Turner. If you scare our woman off I don't think I'll ever be able to forgive you.*

She took a deep, steadying breath and then removed her skirt, and barely held in his gasp of need when he saw she wasn't wearing any undergarments. When she shivered slightly Garth zeroed in on her breasts as did Mac. Her nipples were peaked but only minimally and he realized it was because of the cool air and not in reaction to being topped. Aurora was one of the most petite, sexiest women he had ever seen. Her white-blonde wavy hair cascaded down around her shoulders and back. She had the most expressive green eyes he had ever encountered and her features were delicate, portraying a fragility he was sure was deceptive. Her diminutive height and slight frame made him feel like a veritable giant in comparison.

Garth and Derrick had asked her to play with them previously but she had refused—Turner had told him that right before he and Mike started their duties as dungeon monitors tonight—and he was damn glad she had because he was able to relax more. There was no spark between her and his two Dom friends, at least from her end. She was wrapped up tighter than a spider web and not one Dom in the club had been able to get anywhere near her heart.

"Get on the table on your back, sub," Derrick commanded.

When she was settled, Garth and Derrick set about securing her cuffed wrists and ankles to the rings attached to the bench resembling an exam table and then made sure her restraints weren't too tight by running their fingers beneath the leather.

"What is your safe word, sub?"

"Red, Sir."

"Good, and what word will you use if you need a break from play?"

"Yellow, Sir."

"Very good, Aurora," Derrick praised.

"What are your hard limits?" Garth asked.

"No sex, Sir."

"What does that mean, sub? You don't want penetration at all, or just no sex with us?"

"Sir?"

Derrick moved to the head of the table and looked down at Aurora. "What he's asking is if you will allow toys, sub?"

"Um...I—I..." Aurora squirmed uncomfortably.

"Okay, no sexual play of any kind," Garth said.

"And why is it you don't like sex, sub?"

"I do, Sir. It's just that...I can't explain it."

Mac cursed under his breath when he saw her blink rapidly. She was close to tears and that was the last thing he wanted. He was about to enter the room but a hand on his shoulder stopped him.

"Wait a bit longer and watch," Turner whispered in his ear, and when he looked at the club owner he saw he was watching Mike. A small curl of Turner's lip let him know that his brother's fury amused their friend.

"We are going to use wax play on you, Aurora. Are you agreeable?"

"Yes, Sir." Her response was immediate, almost eager, but her body didn't react at all.

"All right, if things become too much for you, safe word out." Garth looked over at Derrick. His brother's mouth was pulled tight. Mac knew just how he felt. Neither of them wanted to go through with the scene but they had promised Turner to try. "Derrick is going to coat your skin with oil. That way the wax won't be too hard to remove once the wax play has ended."

Garth stood back and watched as Derrick massaged oil into every part of her body. His hands kneaded and shaped Aurora's breasts but her areolas and nipples remained dormant. He avoided touching her pussy as he massaged to oil into her thighs. No twitch or wiggle as his brother's hands ran over her skin. He glanced down to her bare labia and couldn't see any cream coating her lips.

With a sigh of relief he watched Garth move over to his bag and pull out a thick, odorless candle and light the wick while Derrick wiped his hands on a towel and then placed a blindfold over Aurora's eyes. Mac knew the two Doms hoped losing her sight would get to some of her senses. That wasn't about to happen and he wondered how long it would be before Mike broke and took over. Turner gave him a look and he could see the arrogant bastard was enjoying every minute of their torture. If he hadn't figured out what Turner's plan of action was, he knew he would have broken way before Mike. He was less of a control freak than Mike, but he'd had a lot of practice holding back and keeping a tight rein on himself. But where Aurora was concerned, well, that was a totally different story. His gut was churning and he had a knot of pain in his chest which had formed the moment Aurora had undressed. When Derrick had covered his woman's body in oil, if it hadn't been for Turner's presence he knew damn well he would have already been in that room playing with his sub, after kicking the others out first, of course.

When the flame had taken Garth began to work. He drizzled hot wax between her breasts, and all over her fleshy globes, teasing her senses and body by not spilling the wax on her nipples. By now any other sub would have been thrusting their chest up, trying to coax their Master to splash the wax on her nipples, but Aurora lay very still. Her breathing was deep and even, no excited panting at all. No physical response at all.

Mac saw the frustrated sigh building in Garth's chest as he inhaled and barely kept it from escaping his mouth. He looked up as he caught movement through the large glass window when Mike took a step toward the door. Mac and Mike stood staring at Garth and Derrick, and the other Doms didn't look happy. Their muscles were tense and they looked like they wanted to run from him and his brother. He held in a smile when he watched Mike look down at the red armbands around his upper arms proclaiming them as monitors for the moment.

Mac shifted, his arms crossing over his chest, his feet shoulder width apart, and he pinned Garth with his gaze. A quick glance at Mike again and he could literally see steam coming out of his brother's ears.

Oh yeah, definitely pissed.

Garth turned away and watched as Derrick dripped more wax onto Aurora's flat belly and then down her spread thighs. Still no sign of arousal on her pussy and she looked as cool and calm as a cucumber. Mac wondered what she would do if Garth or Derrick removed that blindfold and told her to look out the window. Would she react to seeing him and Mike watching through the glass?

Maybe it was time to find out.

Chapter Five

Aurora thought about the washing she really should have done that day but she was so tired she had put it off. When Derrick had smoothed the oil into her breasts and then the rest of her skin, she had hoped that her body would react in some way. But once again she had felt absolutely nothing. Of course having her breast massaged was pleasant enough, but she didn't feel any great surge of lust or excitement. No tingles had raced down her body to her pussy like she'd heard other subs say had happened to them when they had their breasts played with. A sigh left her mouth when another line of hot wax was poured onto her skin, and other than a little heat from the hot wax, she felt nothing. *What the hell is Master Turner trying to prove? That I am indeed frigid?* Considering she felt nearly numb with boredom she began to think that that may well be the case.

She wondered how long Masters Garth and Derrick would continue with this farce. She sighed with resignation and wondered why Master Turner had bothered asking her to play with these two Doms. Guilt assailed her but there was nothing she could do to make her dormant body respond. Why couldn't she be like all the other subs? Why did she have to be broken inside?

She'd seen a lot of play over the last twelve months and none of the other subs had trouble responding to any of the Doms who played with them. Those boys in high school and college had to have been right. She was totally *frigid*. Tears pricked her eyes and she drew another deep breath, trying to keep her emotions at bay. Aurora was going to end up an old maid with her virginity intact. Maybe she would get a cat or two to keep her company. She quickly vetoed that idea. She'd never had the chance to have pets when she was growing up. Her parents had been too busy to give her the time of day, let alone an animal. She had never had friends over or been allowed to go and spend time with other kids her own age. Aurora had spent the whole of her life alone. And she was still alone. In the end she had stopped trying to make friends. It just hurt too damn much to try and get close to someone and then be rejected time and time again. There had been one girl who Aurora had clicked with in high school. Her name had been Louise. They had spent nearly all their spare time together. But when she'd had to repeatedly refuse the offer to go to Louise's house and refute Louise visiting her home, her friend had given up and they had drifted apart. That had cut her to the bone. It had been too painful to watch Louise interact with other girls and Aurora had finally decided to keep to herself. It was less painful that way and she didn't have to keep disappointing people.

The servants had treated her more like family than her own parents had. They had virtually raised her since her parents were too busy socializing with their elite acquaintances.

It had been a couple of years since she had seen her parents, but it was really no loss, since she'd hardly ever seen them when she was living at home. She could still remember the horror on her mother's face when she had discovered her stash of erotic books. Anyone would think that Aurora had murdered someone with the way her mom had carried on. Her breath hitched as she remembered what had happened next.

* * * *

"Where did you get this trash?" her mom screamed.

"I bought it."

"You what? Are you crazy? What if some of our friends find what you read?"

"So what?" Aurora replied with a shrug. "I don't see how that could happen unless they went rifling through my bedroom."

"What will your future husband think?" her mom wailed. "Wait until your father gets home, young lady. You are in so much trouble."

Aurora couldn't believe the way her mom screeched over what she read. She closed the door after her mom stormed out. She had to finish up the last paper for her last class. She was graduating soon, and that was all that mattered in her mind.

She'd been lucky enough to find a job to walk into which she would start next week. Through school she had worked part-time in a cafe, much to her parents' horror, since they were well-to-do snobs, but she loved meeting other people, and since she was still living at home she had saved every dime she earned. There was a satisfaction at working hard to earn money. She liked working and being rewarded for a job done well. There was no way she could sit at home being bored. Aurora needed to feel fulfilled, as if her life had purpose.

Aurora hadn't wanted to be like her mom, flitting around town getting her nails and hair done every other week and putting stock in the clothes she wore and how perfect she looked at all times. Her dad was too busy making money in the stock market to give her the time of day, and her mom was so shallow she didn't like her very much. Of course she loved her parents, but they were so different Aurora often wondered if she'd been adopted. Or had come from the mailman. She gave a mental snort. Like that would ever have happened. Her mom wouldn't be seen dead with anyone from the lower working class.

That night her father stormed into her room and read her the riot act about how he didn't bring his daughter up to be a slut and how he had such plans for her. He searched her room and found her books, and much to her dismay, he took every book she possessed besides her textbooks and brought them into the backyard. Aurora watched as he burned them to ashes. Her father had started telling her how he had arranged for her to become engaged to one of his colleagues and how he expected her to be a proper wife, just like her mother. She knew *then that nothing she ever did would please her parents, and she began to make plans.*

In the dead of night she crept out of the house, got into a taxi, and went to a hotel. She found an efficiency to lease, and that was that. It was nearly two years since she'd last seen her parents, and they hadn't once tried to contact her. She had taken her cell phone with her and had waited for them to call and apologize but she was still waiting.

* * * *

Warm fingers brushed against her temple, bringing her back to the present. *Shit!* She'd done it again. Her mind had wandered and she hadn't even consciously stayed in the room while two Doms played with her. *What is wrong with me?* she screamed in her head.

"Get her out of the restraints, Derrick," Garth ordered as he went to work on the cuffs at her ankles.

She lifted her head and saw that the wax had been removed from her body. She'd been so wrapped up in her thoughts she hadn't even noticed it. She was a lost cause. From now on the only interaction she would have with a Dom was when she greeted them and signed them in. She was done with the whole Dom/sub stuff since it obviously wasn't right for her after all.

Master Derrick helped her to her feet. "Thank you for trying, Aurora. We know you did your best."

Aurora saw sincerity in his eyes and felt some of the tension and guilt leave her body, but then he gently gripped her shoulders and turned her toward the window. Her breath caught in her throat as her eyes met two sets of male gazes. One a piercing blue and the other a deep, angry aqua color. Her heart stuttered and then pounded out a rapid tattoo inside her chest. She took a step back and bumped into Master Derrick, but she couldn't take her eyes off of them.

Her breasts, which had been unresponsive, began to swell, and her areolas pulled into little ruched bumps. Her nipples ached and became hard as they filled with blood, and her pussy clenched as cream began to leak from her vagina. And then she watched as those two sets of cool blue eyes turned to fiery hot.

She was only vaguely aware of Masters Derrick and Garth exiting the room as Masters Mac and Mike stalked toward her. They perused her naked body from the top of her head to the tips of her toes, stopping in strategic places, which only seemed to ramp up her arousal. Aurora had never felt so turned on, not even when she had read her first BDSM ménage story. She felt like a deer caught in the headlights of an oncoming car, knowing she should move out of the way but too mesmerized to get her body to obey her brain.

They were each decked out in tight black jeans and T-shirts and moved with a masculine, predatory grace. And she felt like she was their prey.

"Kneel, sub," Master Mac ordered.

Aurora found herself obeying and knelt before them in the slave position with her head lowered. Her hands trembled as she placed them palm up on her thighs, but it wasn't with fear or trepidation. It was with arousal.

For the second time in her life Aurora was turned on by two Doms, and not just any Doms, but the two men she had been hankering for, for so long. *Maybe I'm not broken after all.*

Master Mike gripped her hair and tilted her face up. "You can stop this anytime you want, Aurora. You have a safe word and you will use it if you need to."

"Yes, Master." Aurora shivered. Her nipples hardened even more, and juices leaked from her pussy onto her thighs. *Oh God, I'm so turned on. Please, please, please touch me.*

"Rise, sub," Master Mac commanded.

She rose to her feet.

"I want you on the spanking bench, baby."

Another shudder shook her frame, but she found herself walking toward the bench across the other side of the room. How she was able to move on legs that felt like the consistency of wet noodles she had no clue. When she was in position, draped across it, she held still while they secured her wrists and ankles with the cuffs. Her mind raced as she wondered what they were going to do to her. Her body ached to be filled by them, but she wasn't sure she should let them. They had ignored her for so long. Why all of a sudden were they willing to see to her needs now?

"You have been a very bad little sub. Will you take your punishment and please your Doms?" Master Mac asked in a low voice.

"Yes, Master," she responded before she could stop herself. Aurora wanted to ask them why they wanted to play with her now, but knew if she spoke out of turn she would displease the two Doms and earn more punishment.

Warm hands caressed her ass cheeks, and it took everything she had not to wriggle or thrust her ass up into Master Mike's hands.

"Do you know why we're going to punish you, Aurora?"

"No, Master."

Smack. Aurora gasped as a hard hand slapped her ass. The sting radiated heat into her flesh, and the vibrations caused her clit to throb.

"You need to be punished for letting other Doms play with you. If I ever catch you with another man there will be hell to pay, baby." He landed smack after smack on her ass, raining blows on each cheek alternately but never alighting in the same place.

The tension seeped from her body and she became more relaxed with each swat. After the tenth blow, the stinging pain seemed to morph into pleasurable tingles which reverberated from her butt cheeks and traveled around to her pussy. She inhaled deeply and sank into the calm sea of sensation. Her awareness was of her own needy body and the two Doms in the room with her.

Fingers caressed her slit, rubbing through her swollen, wet tissue and up to her engorged nub. *Hallelujah, I have a wet pussy. If I can get turned on then that must mean I'm not frigid.* Her clit throbbed in time with her rapid heartbeat and her cunt clenched as if begging to be filled.

"So fucking wet," Master Mac rasped. "You like getting your ass spanked, don't you, sub?"

"Yes, Master," Aurora replied. *Was that my voice sounding so dreamy and breathy?*

"No one else can make you wet for them, can they, baby?" Master Mike asked as he slapped her ass again.

"No, Master."

"Such an honest little sub." His hands smoothed over her ass cheeks, making them tingle even more.

She sobbed with arousal and hoped they would make her come. She was so hot, wet, and achy, and she knew only these two men would be able to quench the fire burning inside.

"When was the last time you had sex, honey?" Master Mac asked.

"I–I…" Aurora stammered, and then she cried out when a finger drew small circles on top of her clit.

Smack. "Answer the question, Aurora," Master Mike demanded.

"Never, Master."

The hands caressing her ass stopped and the finger massaging her clit halted.

"Are you a virgin, sub?" Master Mac asked in a hoarse voice.

"Yes, Master."

"Fuck me. Send her over, Mac."

The finger working her clit began to rub, starting off slow and gathering speed while the hands on her ass gripped and kneaded it, separating her cheeks and stretching her asshole. Aurora whimpered as another finger rimmed around her pussy, gathering cream and creating blissful pleasure. Then that finger began to penetrate her body and the one on her clit moved faster and faster. Her internal walls rippled, sending more cream to drip from her vagina. Her womb grew heavy and her blood heated as her insides grew tauter and tauter. The further the finger slid inside her cunt, the more her need grew, and she tried to force that digit in more. Another slap landed on her ass, this one much harder than the preceding smacks. She cried out when the finger was withdrawn but then mewled with delight as two were pressed inside her body. Then they began to move. In and out they thrust, stretching and caressing her wet flesh while sending shards of pleasure coursing through her.

The tension inside her grew in mammoth proportions until she felt like she was on the edge looking over the cliff face. And then she was there, right on the precipice, gasping in great gulps of air as she tried to fill her lungs.

Aurora screamed as bliss assailed her from all sides. Fingers rubbed against her asshole, lighting her up, as others pumped in and out of her pussy and rubbed her clit. Her body shook and shuddered as her cunt clamped down on the digits forging their way in and out of her vagina, the strokes never letting up as she hurtled over the side of the cliff. Cum gushed from her sheath and dripped onto her thighs, and her body trembled as rapture caught her in its snare.

She'd never felt anything like what she was experiencing right now. Self-induced orgasms paled into insignificance. When the last contraction faded, Aurora became aware of the soothing hands running up and down her body and over her limbs.

"Such a responsive little sub. You are perfect, baby," Master Mike praised.

Aurora shivered and sighed with relief. Relief at finally knowing she wasn't as cold and frigid as she thought. Master Turner had been right after all. She was a two-men woman and no one else would do. But was she willing to get into a relationship with men who had ignored her for so long? Did they even want a relationship with her? For all she knew they might just want to play and then walk away.

Why didn't they fuck me? Is it because I'm a virgin? Are they turned off because I've never had sex before? Do they only want to play with me because they saw other Doms with me? Why do they want me now after avoiding me for so long? Am I willing to put my heart on the line for these men? Absolutely!

If I don't give them a chance I will always wonder what could have been. For the rest of my life, I would regret not being with them.

Aurora pushed those thoughts aside. She was putting the cart before the horse. Until she knew what they wanted from her, she was just going to have to play it by ear, or go with the flow.

The cuffs were unclipped from the rings and then she was lifted from the bench. She inhaled Master Mac's spicy, fresh cologne and sighed with pleasure, resting her head on his shoulder. A blanket was draped over her body, and she snuggled up against his warm, hard frame. This was the first time he or Master Mike had really touched her and it still wasn't enough. She wanted to be held and loved, to feel their hands and mouths over every inch of her skin, and she wanted to be able to reciprocate by bringing them pleasure with her mouth and hands and body.

Aurora yearned to have them fill her up but not just physically. She wanted the whole nine yards. Tears pricked her eyes but she forced them back. Aurora wanted to be loved unconditionally, but she wasn't sure these two Doms even cared for her. For all she knew she was just someone to scratch an itch.

Chapter Six

Mac felt so content at having Aurora in his arms. When she rubbed her cheek against his chest and sighed with satiation, pride filled him. He and Mike had made their little sub come, and from what he understood, it was a first for her. But what he wanted most of all was to bury his cock inside that hot, wet little pussy.

Both he and Mike were amazed to learn that she was a virgin. He'd felt almost unworthy to be touching such a pure, sweet, innocent woman and had nearly walked away, but that would have left her open for anyone else to make a move on her. That was not going to happen while he had breath left in his body. As far as he was concerned she was theirs. Now all he and Mike had to do was convince her she was meant to be with them.

Mac had wanted to push his jeans down, release his dick, and plunge deep inside Aurora, but her first time shouldn't be in a club for all to see. It should be in a bed where they could take their time and love her the way she should be. He carried her out to one of the semi-secluded seating areas and sat down with her on his lap. She was such a little thing he barely felt her weight as he held her.

Mike sat down beside them and handed him an open bottle of water. Mac placed the rim to Aurora's lips and ordered her to drink. She took a few sips and then sat up a little straighter. The endorphins from their play and her climax were finally waning from her system. She glanced around and then looked at Mike and finally him.

"How are you feeling, honey?"

"Good, Master," she answered, but Mac could hear uncertainty in her voice.

"What's going through that mind of yours, little sub?"

"May I dress now, Master Mac?"

Mac looked at Mike, who was frowning at Aurora. His brother obviously picked up on their sub's worry as well.

"Yes, you can dress, but we need to talk, baby." Mike handed over Aurora's clothes and they both watched as she dressed without being self-conscious. Since she had been working in the club for nearly twelve months, Mac assumed she had become comfortable with nudity. When she was dressed she picked up the water from the small table and took a seat in the armchair across from the sofa.

"What did you want to talk about?" Aurora sipped her drink.

"We would like the chance to get to know you better, and we want you to come home with us for the weekend." Mac leaned back in the sofa.

Aurora frowned, expressions flitting across her face, but she was quite good at concealing her emotions, so he couldn't work out what was going through her mind.

"Why now?" Aurora asked and then placed the bottle back on the table and crossed her arms beneath her breasts.

Uh-oh. Her body language doesn't bode well for us.

Mike leaned forward, resting his elbow on his thighs. "Aurora, there were some issues I needed to work through before we could approach you, which I won't go into here, but suffice it to say, I needed to come to terms with an event which happened in my past which shook my self-confidence. Once I got my head around that, we were free to pursue you."

"Why should I be with you since you've done such a good job at ignoring me?"

"Honey, we know you are as attracted to us as we are to you." Mac clasped his hands together between his legs. "Please, will you give us a chance to get to know you?"

Mac waited with bated breath. He'd never felt so unsure in his life, and that irked him. He was a Dom and full of confidence most of the time, but he felt like he was dangling on the end of a fishhook about to be cast adrift in the wide-open sea. He glanced at Mike and saw that his brother was just as tense as he was. They had screwed up by ignoring Aurora, and her self-confidence had taken a beating because of them.

"If I agree to spending time with you and I don't like what you do to me, will you stop?"

"Your safe words will work the same in our home as they do here at the club," Mike answered.

Mac watched as Aurora's arms unfolded from across her chest. She pushed her shoulders back and took a deep breath. She released it on a sigh. "Okay."

Excitement thrummed through him, warming his blood. His muscles pumped up, and his cock, which had been hard during the scene with her but had deflated to half-mast as they sat talking, surged back to life, pushing against the zipper of his jeans. He rose to his feet and stared into Aurora's beautiful emerald-green eyes. Mike surged to his feet beside him.

"Thank you, Aurora. You won't regret it." Mac held out a hand to her and waited patiently. He and Mike were going to have to be very careful with their little sub. They needed to earn her trust and help her regain her self-esteem. They would do everything within their power to please her over and over again. He knew the next couple of days and nights would either make or break their woman. If they weren't careful they would send their little sub running, and if that happened he didn't think she would give them another chance.

Her little hand touched his palm, and he enfolded hers in his. Her skin was cool to the touch, and his flesh engulfed hers with its size, but nothing had ever felt so right. Mac moved to her other side as he guided her away from the seating area, and his brother took her other hand in his own. They walked her around the dance floor and skirted people, being careful not to bump into anyone. He was a Dom and the need to protect surged in his heart, filling him with pride. There was no way he was about to let Aurora get hurt. Just as they reached the internal double doors to the great room, Master Turner stepped in front of them.

He glanced at Mac and Mike then studied Aurora intently. "Are you sure this is what you want, Aurora?"

Mac glared at Turner, and Aurora stiffened at his side. He hoped she didn't back out. Her little hand trembled in his, and for a second he was worried she would let go and step back. He squeezed her hand, trying to convey comfort and let her know without verbalizing that he would keep her safe.

"Yes, Master Turner."

* * * *

Aurora glanced around the living room and wondered if she was doing the right thing. She looked at the leather sofa and armchairs which had been strategically placed so they faced the wide-screen TV on the wall. The furniture was large and chunky just like the two Doms, but the throw rug on the back of the couch and the pillows on the chairs added a feminine touch and contrasting color. She looked over her shoulder and saw that Mike and Mac were leaning against the wall watching her. Her breath hitched in her throat and her nipples pebbled.

"Take a seat, Aurora." Mike pushed himself away from the wall and moved closer. "Would you like something to drink, baby?"

Aurora sat down on the sofa but on the end, so that only one of them could sit beside her if they chose to. She was still feeling uncomfortable around them and didn't want to feel like she was boxed into a corner. "Coffee would be nice, thank you."

"How do you take it, honey?" Mac asked as he walked toward the door which led to the kitchen.

"Black, please."

"Ah, a woman after my own heart." Mac smiled and disappeared.

Mike sat down on the sofa cushion beside her and clasped her hand. She looked into his light blue eyes and wondered why he looked a little sad. Usually she had trouble reading emotions on Mike. He had perfected that cold, blank stare and granite mask Doms usually wore to a tee.

"Let me explain why we have ignored you," Mike began.

Aurora watched his face as he explained about a sub he had been trying to top. Once he was done she leaned back in the sofa and squeezed his hand. "Thank you for explaining, but…"

"Go on and ask. I'll answer any of your questions."

Mac came back into the living room and placed the mugs of coffee on the table in front of the sofa and then sat in the armchair closest to her.

"Why did you feel okay to play with other subs and not me? From what you've just explained your ego took a battering, which I understand, but why not me?"

"We were too scared to touch you, honey. You're so small and we are fucking huge in comparison. We wanted to, believe me, but we were afraid. You are such a sexy, passionate woman, Aurora, and we are honored that you trust us," Mac answered.

Heat suffused her cheeks and a little of the ice encasing her heart chipped away.

"If it hadn't been for Turner we would probably still be avoiding you," Mike said honestly. "We knew as soon as we saw you all those months ago that we wanted you, but I was too stubborn to pull my head out of my ass. Turner made me open my eyes, plus a little jealousy in the mix didn't hurt."

Aurora giggled and then outright laughed. The image of Mike bent over with his head up his butt was not an image she would have had until now.

"God, you're sexy," Mike said in a raspy voice. "I love the sound of your laughter. You should do it more often."

Aurora ignored the sexy comment, for the moment. "I wondered why Master Turner ordered me to do a scene with Masters Garth and Derrick."

"Manipulative bastard," Mac said with a smile. "Can I ask you something, honey?"

"Sure, but depending on what the question is, I don't know if I'll answer."

"Fair enough." Mac slid from his chair and knelt at her feet, placing his hands on her thighs palms down, and caressed her skin. "Why don't you get aroused for other Doms?"

Aurora drew in a ragged breath. Of all the questions he could have asked, she hadn't seen that one coming. The tension which had seeped from her muscles as they began talking permeated her body once more.

Firm fingers gripped her chin and turned her head. Mike's eyes were cool as he looked at her. "You will answer that question honestly, Aurora, or everything stops now."

Shit! He'd just gone into Dom mode in the blink of an eye. Her eyes slid away, but a slap to her thigh brought them back to connect with his once more.

"Because I'm only attracted to you both."

Mike leaned forward and kissed her lightly on the lips and then wiped the moisture from her face. She was just glad that she was able to stem the flow of tears. She drew in a deep breath.

"Such an honest little sub. Thank you for answering even though you are still holding back. I know there is more to that question, but I'll let it go for now."

Does he know I care for him, for them? No, surely I've hidden my emotions well enough?

After Aurora had finished her coffee, Mike helped her to her feet.

"Remove your clothes, Aurora."

Aurora fumbled with the clasps on her bodice but removed her corset. She folded it neatly and dropped it onto the coffee table. The skirt was next, and then she kicked her shoes off.

Master Mac gasped. "You are fucking gorgeous, honey."

"Head up the stairs and to the room at the end of the hallway, sub," Master Mike directed.

Aurora moved, but everything felt a little surreal. She had been dreaming of these two men for so long, it was hard to believe she was actually here with them in their house. She entered the room and drew in an awe-filled gasp. The room was beautiful and from what she could see the facilities were big enough to hold a party in.

A rustle behind her drew her attention and she turned around. Masters Mike and Mac were in the process of removing their clothes. Mac's T-shirt hit the floor, and Aurora let her eyes wander over his massively muscular chest. His hands dropped to his waist and he popped the button on his jeans and then lowered his zipper. Her eyes were drawn to the massive bulge still hidden by denim and his underwear. He pushed the jeans down over his hips, taking his fitted cotton boxers with them. He was big all over. Although his waist and hips were narrow, his thighs were strong and bulky with muscle. Her eyes snapped back up to the bobbing appendage and the heavy balls between his spread legs. He was thick and long with a slight curve in his shaft.

Aurora nervously licked her lips and backed away. She was a virgin, for crying out loud, and he was massive. There was no way he was coming near her with *that*.

She bumped into a warm body and spun around. Master Mike took a step back and then spread his legs to shoulder width and held his arms out wide. He was just as damn big as his brother. His cock wasn't as long but he looked to be thicker. How could such a confident man have had doubts about his dominance and control? She trusted them both more than any other men she'd met. There was no way in hell either of these two Doms would ever hurt her. Power oozed from his every pore. He was the epitome of an arrogant Dom, and for the moment they were all hers.

But for how long would they want her, just for the weekend or until they got bored with her?

"What just went through that pretty little head, baby?"

Aurora shook her head and lowered her eyes. She knew that was a mistake as soon as his cock came into view again, so she quickly lowered them to the carpet.

Gentle but firm hands cupped her cheeks and lifted her head. Master Mike's stare was implacable and she knew she had to answer, but how to do that without giving her heart away, she had no idea.

"Answer me, sub," he demanded in a hard voice.

"I was just wondering how long this would last."

Master Mike's gaze softened and he kissed her forehead. "To be honest, how can any of us know that right now? I'd like to be able to tell you, but we have a lot to learn about each other. Hopefully a relationship between us will last, but none of us can see the future, baby. Why don't we just take one step at a time?"

Aurora nodded her head. She just hoped that she wouldn't end up heartbroken if they decided they weren't what she was looking for. Large, warm hands landed on her hips and turned her toward the bathroom.

"Let's take that shower, honey. The warm water will help you to relax a little." Master Mac guided her into the bathroom after Master Mike. She waited while Master Mike turned on the shower and adjusted the temperature and was glad that there were multiple showerheads so she wouldn't have to fight for the water.

Master Mike stepped in and then took her hand and gently pulled her in after him. Master Mac also got in and closed the glass door behind him. Aurora wet her hair and reached for the bottle of shampoo above her head, but her arm was gently pulled back down by her side.

"Let us do that, honey." Master Mac began to wash her hair while Master Mike grabbed a cloth and poured some shower gel on it.

The two men washed her from head to toe, and by the time they were finished Aurora was so horny she wanted to jump their bones. Instead she waited patiently while they bathed themselves. Master Mike got out of the shower and dried off, and when he was done Master Mac turned off the water and helped her out. She reached for the towel in Master Mike's hands, but the scowl on his face let her know he wasn't about to relinquish control. When they were done they led her into the bedroom.

"Get on the bed, Aurora."

Chapter Seven

Aurora's breath hitched in her throat as she climbed up on the bed. This was it. This was the night she would lose her virginity. She had begun to think this moment would never happen. But with these two men, the right two men, she was eager to begin. Aurora wanted to initiate their lovemaking but knew if she did she would be punished. Not that she had any clue where to start. She just hoped that she wouldn't make a fool of herself crying or cringing in pain. She'd heard that a woman's first time could be painful and was filled with trepidation.

Master Mike got on the bed near her feet and Master Mac climbed up beside her. Two sets of hands landed on her flesh and began to caress her, but not where she was aching for their touch. It was as if they knew she was nervous and were trying to calm her anxiety.

"We'll go slowly, honey." Master Mac stroked her belly. "If we do anything that is too much then use the word 'yellow.'"

Aurora nodded and then looked down the length of her body as Master Mike began to caress her thighs. The higher his hands got, the faster and harder she panted. Master Mac turned her head and kissed her. She moaned as he swept his tongue into her mouth and devoured her. His tongue slid along hers, and she tentatively copied his moves. Thumbs rubbed in the crease where thigh met groin, and she gasped with pleasure as moisture seeped from her pussy.

Master Mac's tongue explored every inch of her mouth, arousing her to a higher level. Muscular legs nudged hers open, and Master Mike shifted until he was between her splayed thighs. His thumbs moved to her labia and gently pulled them apart. Aurora's sob was muffled by Master Mac's mouth as he ravaged her. Fingers slid through her dripping slit, gathering her cream, and then began to massage her clit.

Master Mac lifted his head and stared down at her. He smiled as if pleased by something, and then he lowered his head and sucked one of her nipples into his mouth while reaching over to pluck the other hard pebble between thumb and finger.

"You're such a passionate little thing," Master Mike panted. "I can't wait to fill your cunt with my cock."

Her pussy clenched and juices leaked out.

"Oh, will you look at that. Our little sub likes dirty talk," Master Mike said.

Aurora groaned as Master Mac leaned over further and sucked her other nipple into his mouth.

"I'm going to lick and suck on every inch of this pretty pussy." Master Mike shifted between her legs.

Aurora felt his breath against her pussy and arched her hips up. A slap landed on her thigh.

"You don't control what happens in the bedroom, sub. We'll give you what you need but in our own good time."

Master Mike lowered his head and licked her from hole to clit and back again, but he didn't stop at her pussy hole. He slid his hands in under her ass and tilted her hips up and then licked her asshole. Aurora whimpered as she was assaulted with pleasure. Until she felt it she wouldn't have believed her ass was so sensitive. He moved back up to her pussy and laved the tip of his tongue over her clit. The urge to cant her hips up into his face was so strong she had to clutch the sheet to stop herself.

Master Mac maneuvered on the bed until he was behind her and she was between his spread thighs. Her upper body was supported by his, and he wrapped his arms around her, cupping her breasts in his big palms.

Master Mike continued licking and sucking on her clit, and she mewled when he began to push a finger into her pussy. His finger was so thick she clenched down hard, not sure if she was trying to keep him out or pull him in.

"Relax, honey. We'll take care of you." Master Mac squeezed her nipples.

The finger slid in and out of her vagina, gaining more depth with each stroke. Aurora felt her internal walls ripple, and cream gushed from her cunt. She sobbed with frustration when Master Mike withdrew his fingers but then nearly sang hallelujah when he pushed back in with two fingers. He started off slowly, but with each press inside he picked up speed and depth. His tongue never stopped working over her clitoris. Heat built in her blood and melted her from the inside out. Aurora felt a slight pinch, but then the small pain faded as Master Mike eased his fingers back. He held his digits still inside her and flicked his tongue over her little pearl rapidly. Her legs began to tremble, as did her belly, and her internal walls gathered in. The tension grew tighter and tighter until she was about to burst.

And then she did. Aurora threw her head back and screamed as pleasure assailed her from all sides. Her nipples throbbed, and little sparks of electricity zinged from her breasts to her clit as Master Mac pinched them hard. That small bite of pain was enough to send her over the edge. Discomfort radiated from her pussy as Master Mike thrust his fingers into her hard and deep, but then the pain changed to bliss. Wave upon wave of rapture swept over her. Cream gushed from her sheath as continuous contractions erupted inside. Her pussy clamped down on the fingers inside and then released. Master Mike continued to thrust in and out until the last tremor faded away. Aurora gasped for breath and slumped down onto Master Mac.

Master Mike sat up between her legs and wiped her juices from his mouth and chin. "Your cream is fucking delicious, baby. I can't wait to get inside that pretty little pussy." He leaned forward and kissed her ravenously. When he lifted his head they were both breathing heavily.

Master Mike moved closer and she looked down to see he was gripping the base of his cock in his hand. He pumped his fist up and down his shaft a few times, and when she saw the pearl glistening on the tip of his penis, she licked her lips, wondering what he tasted like.

"Are you ready for me, baby?"

"Yes, Master Mike. Please?"

"Please what, little sub?"

"Please make love to me?"

"My pleasure, Aurora."

After Master Mike rolled a condom onto his cock, he pushed his groin forward, until the tip of his penis began to separate her flesh. She groaned and dug her nails into Master Mac's forearms.

"Don't move, baby. I don't want to hurt you." Master Mike groaned as the head of his dick popped through her entrance.

He took his time, advancing and then holding still, letting her body adjust to his intrusion, but Aurora wanted him deep inside. She sobbed with need and thrust her hips up. A slap landed on her pubis.

"Don't fucking move," Master Mike said through clenched teeth.

Aurora froze and looked up to see a tortured expression on Master Mike's face. Sweat beaded on his forehead, and she knew he was trying to be gentle with her, but since she had felt him break through her hymen as he finger-fucked her, she didn't understand why he kept a tight rein on his control. Her expression must have shown her confusion.

"Yes, I broke through your barrier, baby, but if I'm too rough with you you'll be even sorer. This is your first time, Aurora, and I want it to be special."

Warmth filled her chest and the ice around her heart melted even more. She felt so warm and fuzzy inside, almost cherished.

Master Mike took his time, and when he was embedded in her balls-deep, she was ready to scream at him to fuck her. She bit her lip and inhaled several times, trying to regain control over her needy body. Just when she thought she'd lose it, Master Mike began to move. He eased his cock from her pussy until just the tip was inside, and then he surged back in. With each stroke inside he sped up until his balls were tapping her ass and the front of his thighs slapped against the back of hers. Aurora moaned, rolling her head against Master Mac's chest as the pleasurable friction inside began to build.

Master Mac nibbled across her shoulder and up her neck until he reached her ear. He sucked her earlobe into his mouth and nipped gently, and then he traced the rim with his tongue. His breath caressed her skin, causing her to shiver with joy.

The fire building inside her flamed to new heights as Master Mike pumped his hips faster and harder. The tightness became tauter and tauter until she knew she was on the edge of orgasm again. She tried to hold it off, to push it back, but it was too big to control. She could feel herself hurtling toward the stars and she didn't know how to stop it.

Master Mike bent slightly and lifted her legs into the crooks of his arms. The new position allowed his cock to gain more depth, and as he thrust in and out of her pussy the head of his dick massaged over a really sensitive spot inside. Aurora cried out and then keened as he passed over what she suspected was her G-spot again and again. The bliss built and built and built and then she screamed as she exploded. Stars formed before her eyes as her body shook and shuddered with the most intense climax of her life. She was only vaguely aware of Master Mike shouting as he, too, reached his peak. His cock jerked inside her, causing her pussy to clench again, and then she felt his warm cum fill the condom.

Aurora panted, trying to calm her breathing and heart rate back to a normal level. Just as they began to even out Master Mike kissed her hard and fast.

"Thank you for trusting me, us, baby. You've given us a wonderful gift."

Both Masters caressed and soothed her until she flopped down onto Master Mac supine with satiation. Master Mac thrust his hips into the small of her back. The hard ridge of his cock pulsed against her skin. Aurora groaned, not sure if she would survive another round of lovemaking but wanting more than anything for Master Mac to make love with her, too.

* * * *

Mac was so on edge he didn't know if he would be able to get fully inside Aurora's pussy before shooting off. Watching her as Mike made love to her had been one of the most beautiful, sexiest things he had ever seen. Mike held the condom and gently withdrew from her pussy and then headed to the bathroom.

Mac felt so humbled that she trusted them enough to gift them with her innocence. He vowed to do everything he could to keep her at their sides. He and Mike had been attracted to Aurora from the start, and he knew it wouldn't take much for him to fall in love with her. He was already halfway there. If only Mike had spoken to Turner sooner, then they may already have had the grounds for a relationship. He pushed those thoughts aside because he couldn't turn the clock back.

Mac gripped Aurora beneath her arms and pulled her further up his body and then rolled until she was beneath him. He got up on his knees and then flipped her over onto her back. If this wasn't his first time with her he would have taken her doggy style, but because it was, he wanted to watch her face as he made love to her. He leaned forward and consumed her mouth as he ran his hands over her body. When she moaned and wiggled and then arched her hips up he knew she was ready. He dipped his fingers into her pussy and found her soaking wet. After donning a condom he pushed inside her hot, tight vagina.

His groan merged with hers, and he rocked his hips forward and back with slow, gentle strokes until he was fully inside her. Her muscles clenched and released, stroking his cock and sending him to the edge, but he stilled and breathed in and exhaled, slowly regaining control of his raging arousal. Shifting his arms and legs, he lowered his body over hers, blanketing her with his large frame. Sliding his hands under her ass, he nudged her legs wider with his thighs and began to surge in and out of her pussy.

Never had he felt anything like what he was right now. She reminded him of heaven and home. He pumped his hips faster, twisting them slightly as his groin slapped against hers, knowing his pubic bone massaged her clit. Her cunt rippled and squeezed and he mentally cursed when he felt the warning tingle at the base of his spine and his balls drew up closer to his body.

Leaving his hands beneath her ass, he gripped the fleshy globes and lifted more onto his knees. His body was curved over hers with his chest flush with hers, but in this position he had more control over his cock. He pressed forward, going deeper than before, and the corona of his dick butted against her cervix. His little sub must have liked that little bump of pain because she whimpered and tried to shove her hips up to meet his. With each thrust he sped up incrementally until their flesh slapped together. He slanted his mouth over hers and ate her lips and tongue hungrily.

Aurora's cunt clutched at his cock and he was right on the precipice and didn't know if he could hold off. He sat up between her legs and looked over at Mike, who was lying on his side next to her.

"I'm not gonna last," he panted. "Help her over."

Aurora turned passion-glazed eyes to Mike and looked surprised to see his brother on the bed beside her. He was glad she hadn't realized he was there because that meant she was caught up in him and his lovemaking, just like he wanted her to be.

Mike engaged her mouth in a hot kiss, using lips, tongue, and teeth to enhance her pleasure as he slid a hand down her belly to the top of her mound. His brother tapped her clit a couple of times and then began to rub hard and fast.

Aurora mewled and drew her head away from Mike to gulp in air. Her neck arched and her eyes closed when Mac felt her pussy quiver around his cock.

"Look at me, honey," he rasped.

Aurora's eyes met him and then he took a deep breath. "Come now, Aurora."

She screamed with pleasure as her pussy clamped down on his thrusting cock and then released. Her cunt continued to clench and let go, and she coated his dick with her cream as she came. Mac pumped into her one, two, three, four more times and then froze with his cock buried in her depths. He roared as the strongest orgasm he'd ever experienced battered him from all sides. When the last quake waned from her body, Mac slumped down over her, glad that Mike had moved aside so he could cuddle with their sub. He wrapped his arms around her waist and clung to her while he buried his face against her neck and shoulder. When his breathing slowed and his legs stopped shaking, he lifted his head.

Aurora's eyes were closed, her breathing had evened out, and she had a smile on her face. She looked so peaceful while she slept and if he could have stayed buried in her depths he would have, but he needed to take care of his sub. Her care came first and foremost.

Mac held the condom and pulled his cock from her pussy. His legs felt weak but he got off the bed and headed for the bathroom. Once he cleaned up he wet a cloth and walked back to the bedroom. Mike lifted one of her legs and he set about making their little sub more comfortable. When he was done he threw the cloth on the floor and got into bed beside her and pulled the covers up.

"She's perfect, Mike." Mac was careful to keep his voice low so he wouldn't disturb Aurora from her slumber.

"Yes, she is," Mike sighed. "I really screwed up with her. She's still holding back from us."

"I know, but it's better that we started out slow. I didn't want to go all Dom on her for her first time."

"Me either. Do you think she'd agree to stay here after the weekend?"

"No. That's too fast. We need to give her time to get to know us," Mac answered Mike. Once his brother made up his mind he got impatient. He was going to have to make sure Mike didn't screw up by pushing Aurora too quickly. The last thing they needed was to have her running scared. She was already nervous about letting them in. Mac only hoped that they would be able to get through to her by the end of the weekend.

He knew without a doubt that Aurora was the one for them. Now all they had to do was convince her that they were right for her, too. Hopefully she would learn to trust them and open her heart, but if she didn't, then they were screwed.

Chapter Eight

Mike watched Aurora as she ate her breakfast. For such a little thing she had a voracious appetite. He loved that she ate with such gusto and didn't worry about her weight. Not that she needed to because she was so damn petite already, but he would love it if she put on a few pounds. Although he liked Aurora fine just the way she was it wouldn't hurt her to carry a little extra weight. He pushed her mug of coffee within reach as she shoved her plate aside. She had responded to them so openly and honestly, but he knew she was still holding back from them. It was going to take time before she trusted them fully and let them in, but he hoped that she would let them be around when that happened. The thought of another man touching her, loving her, caused anger to churn in his gut and a bubble of pain to form in his chest.

He pushed those thoughts away and remembered what it was like to wake up with her in their bed. If he had anything to say about it she would be living with him and Mac for the rest of her days, but he kept those thoughts to himself.

"Thanks for breakfast." Aurora stood and began to gather the dishes. Mike stood to help her.

"So…" Aurora paused. "What do you do for a living?" she asked with a giggle.

"We own a moving company."

"Wow. That would be great."

"What would be, honey?" Mac asked as he brought more dishes over to the sink.

"To be the boss," she replied and then turned to look over her shoulder to give Mac a cheeky grin.

"Yeah, it's good not having to answer to anyone but ourselves."

"Well, I can definitely see you two giving orders easily enough."

"Oh you can, can you?" Mike grinned at her and then winked.

"How long have you been in the moving business and how did you get into it?"

"Before we served in the Marines we used to work with a moving company on weekends to earn some extra cash while we went through college." Mike paused. "We actually enjoyed the physical labor and liked meeting people and hearing about their stories.

"Once we got out of the military we had enough cash to buy a moving company which was selling up since the owner was retiring. It took us a couple of years to establish ourselves and we did a lot of the work ourselves first up. But now we have good employees whom we trust and can rely on. Occasionally we'll get out and help out but most of our time is spent booking jobs, maintaining our trucks, and making sure everything runs smoothly."

"Sounds nice," Aurora sighed wistfully.

"Do you like your job, honey?" Mac asked.

"Yes, I do." Aurora glanced away when she answered.

Mike knew in an instant that Aurora was ashamed of her job. He reached over, gently gripped her chin, and turned her face toward him. "You have nothing to be ashamed of, Aurora. You work at an honest job to earn your living, baby. Why would you be ashamed of that?"

She turned her head away from him, dislodging his hand, and then gave a slight shrug. Mike thought that he'd heard her talking to Turner about a degree and wondered why she wasn't utilizing that skill but decided not to ask just now. Mike could tell she was uncomfortable so he dropped the subject. When she knew them better, then he and Mac could grill her more.

Just as they finished up the dishes his cell phone rang. He moved away from the kitchen and into the living room, glanced at the display, and saw that the number was restricted for privacy and answered. Mike didn't get the chance to say anything. The masculine voice on the other end of the line was unfamiliar but also sounded like it was being disguised by a computer of some sort.

"You and your brother need to leave town. If you don't, your woman will suffer." The call disconnected before he could reply. He mentally cursed because this wasn't the first call he and Mac had received from the unknown caller, but it was the first time the asshole had threatened anyone but him or his brother.

When he walked back into the kitchen his eyes immediately went to Aurora. The tension he hadn't known he held released from his body slightly. Mac saw how worried he was.

"What's going on?"

"Uh, I just got another call." He didn't have to explain because he knew Mac would immediately know what he was talking about.

"Shit. I'm sick of this asshole. I wish he would just say what his problem is and be done with it."

"What are…"

"He added to the threat." Mike glanced toward Aurora and then looked back at Mac.

"You mean…" Mac gave a slight nod of his head and Mike hoped Aurora hadn't noticed.

"Fuck. That's it. I've had enough of this shit. I'm calling Gary Wade." Mac was pulling his cell phone out of his pocket as he left the room.

"I think that would be best." Mike walked over to Aurora and then pulled her into his arms.

She held herself stiffly for a moment and then wrapped her arms around his waist. Mike breathed in her clean scent and looked down. The top of her head only reached the middle of his chest. He could hurt her so easily. Mike vowed to be as gentle as he could with her and hoped to God she never had reason to yell at him for hurting her.

"What's going on?" Aurora eased back out of his arms.

"Come and sit down, baby." Mike guided her toward the table and then went back to the kitchen to pour them both a cup of coffee. "It seems we may have put you in danger, Aurora."

"What? How?"

"We've been getting threatening calls for a few weeks and we've also had someone break into our house and our warehouse. We've already updated security, as well as the locks to the doors and windows, but until we know who is after us and why, we are totally blind." Mike sighed and then placed his hand on top of hers where it was lying on the tabletop. "I just got another call and the asshole threatened you."

"Me, how could he do that? I've never been with you before."

Mike scrubbed a hand over his face in frustration. "Whoever this person is, they don't know your name, baby, but they do know you are here. The last time I called Gary I let him know that we were being watched." He wanted to bundle Aurora up, shove her into his truck, and drive her someplace safe, but he couldn't do that. Whoever was after him and Mac was watching and for all he knew would take them out as soon as they left the house. He could get her to hide on the floor of his truck, but if the asshole managed to shoot him from long range then Aurora could get hurt when he crashed the car. No, the best thing to do was sit tight.

"Oh shit," Aurora whispered and the blood drained from her face. "They have to be watching right now."

Mike gripped her hand and gave a little rub, and then he pulled her onto his lap and wrapped himself around her. She trembled in his arms, but then the shaking slowed and she lifted her head from his shoulder.

"Gary's on his way," Mac said as he entered the kitchen. He crouched down in front of Aurora and cupped her cheek. "Are you okay, honey?"

"Yeah, I'm fine."

Mike knew she was anything but fine. He could feel the little trembles running through her body, but it seemed their little sub was putting on a brave face. But inside he was also feeling fear. The last thing he and Mac had wanted was for Aurora to be targeted by whoever had a grudge against them. What irked him the most was that he and Mac had no idea why they were being targeted or by whom.

"Don't you worry, honey." Mac leaned over and took her hand in his. "We'll do everything we can to protect you."

Twenty minutes later the doorbell rang. Mac went to let Detective Gary Wade into the house. He smiled at Aurora and then sat down at the table. "Have you got any coffee left?"

"I'll get it." Aurora rose and headed over to the kitchen, poured them all a fresh cup of coffee, and came back, but sat in her own seat this time.

"Where are Tank and Emma?" Mike asked.

"We thought it best that Emma stay home with Tank and Jack this morning. I didn't want anyone seeing her here."

"Fair enough," Mac said.

"Thanks, honey." Gary turned toward him and Mac. "All right, start at the top and don't leave anything out."

Mike and Mac explained about the phone calls and their suspicion of the breaking and entering into their home, as well as the more obvious break-in at the warehouse and the destruction of their office and the graffiti. When they were done Gary began to ask questions.

"Who have you pissed off? Did you make any enemies while you served in the military?"

"No," Mac sighed with exasperated frustration. "We've thought back and can't come up with one reason why someone has it in for us."

"How about your business? Have you had to fire any employees?"

"Yeah, there was one guy. He was such a lazy prick. The other guys were complaining about how they were practically carrying him on the job."

Gary pulled out a notepad and pen. "Give me his name."

"Russell Green."

"Okay. I'll check him out. Give me a call if you think of anyone else." Gary turned to Aurora. "Aurora, is there anyone in your past that could be causing you problems?"

Mike watched as Aurora thought through if she could have an enemy as well. She was frowning and he could clearly see the wheels of her mind working. "Not that I'm aware of."

"Good." Gary rose to his feet and headed out. He gave Mike and Mac a firm stare. "Take care of your woman."

Mac followed Gary out and Mike could hear the deep rumble of his brother's voice, but was glad his words weren't audible. He would be as pissed off as him at Gary's last statement. Neither of them were about to let Aurora get hurt by someone after them.

He brought his attention back to Aurora when she stood and snagged an arm around her waist, pulling her down onto his lap. "Whoa, where are you going, baby?" When she ignored his question and continued pushing at his arm, he let her go with a sigh.

She rose to her feet and began to pace and then turned to face him. "I think I should just go home."

Mike stood up and walked toward her but didn't get too close. The last thing he wanted was for her to feel crowded. "Why?" he asked in an almost snap and then sighed, trying to control his churning emotions. He was going to end up pissing her off if he wasn't careful.

"You have so much going on. I don't think this is a good time to start a relationship."

"Why the hell not?" Mac snarled as he entered the kitchen, obviously having heard Aurora's last statement.

"I just think that you need time to deal with this…enemy you have."

"That's not the reason you want to back off though, is it, baby? You're just using that as an excuse." Mike moved closer and tilted her head up until she was looking into his eyes. "What's really going on, Aurora?"

* * * *

Aurora stared into Mike's eyes and tried to remember what the question was. She wanted to stay with him and Mac, but she had been alone and independent for so long, she was scared of trusting them. Everyone who had ever loved her ended up leaving her or not liking who she was. She had never had the chance to connect to another person. Being scared to create friendships in case her friends walked away was just too much to bear. She'd learned early on that she wasn't the type of person to engender someone to really care about her, to love her. There was something broken inside her that even her own parents hadn't been able to love her.

Even her own family had abandoned her when she didn't fall into their plans of marrying her father's colleague. She couldn't believe how her tyrannical father had tried to arrange for her to marry a stranger, someone she'd never met and didn't even know the name of. And when she had taken off, her parents had obviously wiped her from their lives.

Why am I so unworthy? Why can't anyone love me for who I am? Am I such a bad person? What have I ever done to warrant such treatment?

There was no way she would be able to handle them using her body and entrenching into her heart deeper and then leaving her by the wayside. Well, she was just glad she hadn't spilled her guts and told them she was beginning to care for them.

"I–I just don't think that now is a not good time."

"You're lying," Mike said. He reached up and gripped her chin and stared into her eyes. "Did you know that when a person lies their body gives them away?"

Aurora jumped when Mac pressed his body against her back. She had been so intent on Mike she hadn't been aware of him moving away from the door. Mac's hands gripped her hips and his thumb caressed over her hip bones, causing shivers to race up and down her spine. She tried to hold in the shudder of awareness but knew she hadn't succeeded when Mike narrowed his eyes at her.

It was one of the hardest things that she had ever done but she held Mike's stare. Her insides were shaking and jumping with nervous anxiety, but she was determined to leave. She didn't want them to feel obligated to keep her around because some crazy person was after them. She wasn't their responsibility. Her care and safety was up to her as far as she was concerned. The last thing she wanted to be was a burden. She wanted to be accepted and loved without having to change who she was. Aurora turned her head, dislodging Mike's hand from her chin, and tried to move out from in between them, but her two men weren't about to let her go.

Mac tightened his grip on her hips and Mike wrapped an arm around her waist. "You aren't going anywhere, Aurora. You're already in danger. Do you think we are going to let you go back to your place where you'll be alone and in even more danger?"

She pushed against his arm and was surprised when he released her. Mac withdrew his hands from her hips and she was able to step out from between them. "Look," she snapped and then took a deep breath when Mike narrowed his eyes at her tone. She then released it, trying to get her frustration under control. "I appreciate that you want to look out for me, but I'm used to taking care of myself. I don't need you two looking out for me."

Mac walked right up to her and she gave a squeak of surprise when he gripped her hips and lifted her up, her ass landing on the kitchen counter. He pinned her with his gaze. "We don't give a damn about how long you've been alone and independent. You aren't going to put yourself in danger, little girl. We will be making sure you stay safe."

She looked into Mac's determined gaze and then glanced over as Mike came up on her side. He looked just as indomitable as his brother, if not more so, and even though she wanted to stay with them she knew she would only fall in love with them as time went on. Aurora didn't want to feel any deeper for them than she already did, because she knew just like everyone else who had entered her life and left that these two men would do the same, and she didn't think she could survive without them by her side.

"What are you so damn scared of?" Mike asked.

She mentally cringed at his question, thinking she'd been able to hide her insecurities and uncertainties, but she must have given herself away somehow.

Fucking Doms. Why do they have to see everything?

"I–I'm not scared," she said on a breathy sigh as she looked away.

Mac placed his hands on her cheeks and held her head gently but firmly, giving her no chance to escape or look away again. "We know you are lying, Aurora. What we want to know is why?" He released her face and took a step back, and Mike moved in and swept her up into his arms.

"I've had enough of you trying to hide yourself from us," he said as he walked out of the kitchen and down the hall. "You are going to open up to us if it's the last thing you do."

Mac brushed past them and hurried down the hall. He stopped at the closed doorway and used a key to unlock it. Aurora drew in a ragged breath when he disappeared into the darkened interior, and then she was being carried through the entrance. A light flickered and then illuminated the room. Her breath caught in her throat, and she wriggled in Mike's arms, trying to get down, but she should have known the futility of the act. His arms tightened around her legs and shoulders as he carried her into the middle of what looked like a dungeon.

Chapter Nine

Aurora held on to Mike's forearm as he lowered her feet to the floor. When she was steady on her feet he released her, stepped back, and stood next to Mac. They both eyed her from head to toe, and when their gazes met hers, they were full of heat.

"Strip," Mike commanded.

Aurora was wearing one of Mac's T-shirts which came to her knees and a pair of Mike's boxers since his sweatpants had been way too big to stay on her hips and her own underwear.

After making love with both men last night, she had expected them to rest up a bit and then make love to her again, but they had snuggled with her and must have fallen asleep. She'd been aware of their presence on and off throughout the night. It had been so nice waking up between them this morning and she could envisage being happy to do so again and again.

But now it seemed the two Doms wanted to play. But as she looked at them she realized that Mike was serious. He wanted her to open up and reveal her innermost self, and she wasn't sure that was such a good idea.

Aurora didn't know how to open up to anyone. She'd never really had the opportunity and she'd never trusted anyone with her true personality or her heart's desires. She was so broken inside and even though she cared a lot for the two Doms, she didn't know how to love. How could she when no one had ever shown her any love? Would they still want her when they realized she wasn't worthy of their attention? If her parents couldn't be bothered to notice her, love her, then why would anyone else?

"That's one," Master Mike snapped out.

"The longer you hesitate to obey, the more punishments you are going to rack up, little sub." Master Mac moved closer and tilted her chin up so she could see his eyes. "What's your safe word, honey?"

"Red."

"That's two," Master Mike said in a firm, cold voice.

She drew in a deep breath when she saw that his eyes had turned from hot and hungry to ice cold. She hadn't deliberately forgotten to use the proper address of respect for Master Mac. It was just that being out of the familiar club environment felt a little surreal to her, even if she was in a private dungeon. Since she didn't want to add to the two punishments she already had coming, Aurora reached for the hem of the shirt and pulled it up over her head. Instead of dropping it or folding it and placing the material off to the side, she held it in front of her breasts, trying to hide her naked vulnerability. It wasn't that she would be naked in front of the two Doms that made her feel vulnerable. She was uncomfortable because she felt like she was stripping some of her armor away, chipping away at the thin layer of ice encasing her heart, and she wasn't sure how she felt about that.

"You've just hit number three, baby. Are you deliberately trying to push the number of punishments higher?" Master Mike asked.

"No, Master," Aurora finally managed to answer the way a sub was supposed to. The two Doms intimidated the hell out of her and she had lost the use of her brain. Her heart was racing with a mix of fear and arousal, her body ready for anything they wanted to dish out, but her emotions were all over the place as her mind warred with her body.

"Give me the shirt, honey," Master Mac demanded as he held out his hand. Aurora passed it over and lowered her arms to her sides.

"Remove the shorts, baby." Master Mike stood before her with his arms crossed over his massive chest, and as her eyes drifted down his body they snagged on the prominent bulge at his crotch. The two men always seemed at complete control over themselves, but their bodies gave them away just as hers did. At least she wasn't the only one turned on.

Aurora pushed the boxers down over her hips and stepped out of them. She was left standing in her bra and panties. Again she hesitated to remove the last barriers from her body.

"That's four," Master Mac said in a cool voice, and then he quickly moved forward, bent down, and flipped her over his shoulder. Aurora decided that fighting him would be futile since he was so much bigger and stronger than she was, so she clutched a handful of T-shirt and hung on. She tried to see where he was taking her, but her hair cascaded over her face, blocking her view. It wasn't long before she found out.

She was gently pulled from his shoulder only to find herself facedown over his lap when he sat on an armless chair. One hand was planted in the middle of her back to hold her still while three other large, warm, masculine hands divested her of her underwear. She drew in a ragged breath when slightly abrasive, callused flesh smoothed over the cheeks of her ass. Turning her head to the side was enough movement to move the hair from her face, and she saw the black boots standing close to her and Master Mac.

A stinging slap landed on one cheek, and she gasped as tingling warmth permeated her flesh and traversed to her clit, causing it to throb. Her pussy clenched and fluid began to seep from her vagina.

"Count them out for me, sub," Master Mike commanded in a husky voice.

"One, Master."

"Very nice, Aurora," Master Mac praised. The hand on her back rubbed slightly.

Smack. Smack. Smack. Smack.

"Five, Master Mike," Aurora gasped out through pants. Her skin tingled and heated with each blow, and each time Master Mike's hand landed on her ass the ferocity increased until she was in danger of coming. After the last swat, Master Mike kept the palm of his hand on her butt, holding in the heat of the sting. Cream leaked out onto her thighs and she squeezed her legs together, trying to circumvent the ache in her pussy, but it didn't help. If anything it only seemed to heighten the relentless ache deep inside her cunt.

"Spread those legs right now, sub." Master Mac gripped one of her thighs and applied pressure until she complied with his will.

Smack. Smack. Smack. Smack. Smack.

"Ten, Master Mike," she sobbed.

Firm hands kneaded the globes of her ass, inciting more pleasure-pain to erupt over her sensitive skin. Aurora tried to stay still but her body's instincts took over and she found herself pushing her ass up into their touch.

Smack.

"You don't have permission to move, Aurora. Stay still," Master Mike snapped out in a cold voice.

Aurora inhaled and let her body go lax, but when her ass cheeks were pried apart, every muscle in her body tautened once more.

"You are going to learn to trust us, honey," Master Mac said as he turned her in his arms. He placed an arm beneath her knees and the other around her shoulders, then rose to his feet and walked away from the chair. Aurora wrapped an arm around his neck for balance and then gasped when she saw where he was heading.

Within minutes she was draped over a padded spanking bench with her wrists and ankles restrained, a large strap across her back just beneath her shoulder blades and another across the top of her hips. She pulled on the restraints and arched her body, testing how much movement she had. The fur-lined straps were tight but not enough to hurt her by digging into her skin. She was at their complete mercy with her ass and pussy on display, and even though she didn't want them to know how she felt about them, she wanted their Dominance as well as their hands and mouths touching her nearly more than her next breath.

"Look at the ripe pink peach of an ass," Master Mac said in a growly voice. "It's so small and tight. I can't wait to sink my cock into that tight little hole."

Aurora whimpered with desire as the image of Master Mac preparing her and then sinking his hard cock into her assailed her mind. As much as she wanted to experience everything with these two men, she was also scared about doing something so carnally naughty. She was worried that having a cock shoved up her ass would hurt and she would have to use her safe word. That was something she hoped she never had to do, at least with these two Doms. As those thoughts crossed her mind, Aurora realized she trusted these two men more than she had trusted anyone else in her life, including her parents.

If she didn't she wouldn't have become aroused at the club when they had taken over from Masters Garth and Derrick. She wouldn't be in their home if she didn't trust them and she never would have let them make love to her if trust wasn't involved. If her body trusted them then why couldn't her mind? Then she realized that her mind trusted them as well. Mike and Mac had put themselves on the line for her by telling her of the incident with the sub, Karen, and how they had lost self-confidence because of that. If they didn't care for her a least a little then they would never have opened up to her that way. They had opened up to her more than she had. Aurora realized she stayed closed tight like a locked vault. Would she ever find the courage to really let go? She wasn't sure if she knew how.

Warm fingers slid through the folds of her pussy, caressing and stroking everywhere but where she wanted and needed them the most. They skirted around the nub of her clit and avoided her pussy hole. She sobbed with frustration as every other part of her genitalia was explored.

"You are so fucking wet, Aurora," Master Mike groaned. "I can't wait to fuck this pretty little cunt, but you have three more punishments coming before we can make love with you."

Aurora mewled as those fingers continued to tease her without giving her any relief. Just as she was about to scream that they fuck her, the fingers withdrew from her pussy. Her forehead smacked onto the padded bench and she sucked in great lungfuls of air as she tried to get her raging libido back under control. She listened intently as they moved around and wondered what her next punishment would be. The wait seemed almost interminable but she knew that it had to have been mere seconds that passed.

"Count for me, sugar." Master Mac's demand was the only precursor she got before her ass lit up like the Fourth of July.

Slam.

"One, Master Mac," she sobbed as fire radiated against her ass after the paddle connected with her flesh.

Slam.

"Two, Master Mac."

Slam. Slam. Slam.

"Five, Master Mac." Aurora whimpered and sniffed as tears streamed down her face. Never before had she felt such pleasure and pain. The combination had her body and mind so confused, and endorphins began to flood through her system.

She heard the paddle drop to the tile floor with a loud clatter and moaned with frustration. Aurora was so close to climaxing and wanted to scream at Master Mac to hit her again, but she held her voice and bit her lower lip instead.

When hands began to smooth over her throbbing, hot ass, she groaned and more tears leaked out of her eyes. Her vagina rippled and clenched, causing more of her juices to weep from her pussy and coat the inside of her thighs.

"You're such a good girl, Aurora. I love seeing you submit so beautifully."

Warmth filled her heart at Master Mac's praise, and she knew she would take anything he and Master Mike dished out. She wanted to please them more than anything else.

Heavy footsteps moved away and she heard rustling and popping, like a package was being opened. Then her ass cheeks were pulled apart and held open. She tried to clench, the act of having her most intimate hole exposed leaving her feeling vulnerable and open.

"Don't clench, baby. Try and relax. We won't hurt you, Aurora."

"What's your safe word, honey?" Master Mac asked.

"Red, Master."

"Good girl."

"What word do you use if you are unsure of something, baby?" Master Mike queried.

"Yellow, Master."

"Such a good little sub."

Aurora flinched when cold liquid dribbled into the crack of her ass and down onto her anus. She breathed deeply and tried to keep her muscles lax. Firm but gentle fingers massaged the sensitive skin of her asshole, and she couldn't contain her mewl of delight. She never would have suspected that having her anus touched could bring such pleasure. Then she jerked and cried out as a thick finger pushed into her tight hole, and of course the first thing she did was clench, trying to keep it out.

Smack.

"If you don't stop clenching I'm going to shove ginger up your ass, sub," Master Mac declared.

Fuck! Aurora had heard about figging. Ginger root was used to train a sub to keep her ass muscles loose. If a sub clamped down on the ginger while it was shoved up their ass the burn soon taught the consequences of such an action. Although the ginger caused fire to radiate in the sub's ass, there was no damage, permanent or otherwise, done to the sub, but it wasn't a pleasant experience, so she had been told.

She panted and concentrated hard on keeping her muscles loose, and by the time the finger in her ass was in as far as it could go she was on the verge of climax. When the finger was withdrawn from her ass, she couldn't prevent a groan of disappointment escaping her mouth.

The popping noise sounded again, and then she felt pressure on her rosette again. But this time it wasn't a finger. Cold, hard plastic began to push into her back entrance and she knew that a dildo or anal plug was being inserted into her anus. As the plastic gained more depth with each shunt into her body, her ass began to burn as the muscles were spread apart. Cream was dripping from her pussy in a continuous stream, and her inner thighs were slick with her juices. Just when she didn't think she could take any more pain and she opened her mouth to use the word "yellow," the burning changed to pleasure as the widest part of the plug pushed through the tight ring of muscles. Four hands caressed her lower back, burning bottom, and legs, and those caresses were enough to help settle her once more.

"You have two more punishments coming, baby. We are going to fuck you until we come, but you aren't allowed to climax. Is that understood?" Master Mike asked.

Fucking bastard!

"Yes, Master Mike."

"Such a courteous little sub. You please me, Aurora." Master Mike moved in close and then blanketed her back with his front. She wondered when he had removed his clothes.

Footsteps sounded close to her head, and then the head of the bench was being lowered. Master Mac stood before her totally naked, too. His thick, long cock was too close to her mouth, which all but tempted her to stick her tongue out and lick the head, but she waited for his command, not wanting to add to her contraventions. He crouched down in front of her and lifted her head slightly. "I want you to suck my cock until I come, honey, and you will swallow every drop I give you. Okay?"

"Yes, Master," she answered breathily and unconsciously licked her lips.

Master Mac moved in close and then slanted his mouth over hers. By the time he lifted his mouth they were both gasping for breath. He stood up straight and then moved in as close as he could, which put his cock right in alignment with her mouth. With the head of the bench gone all she had to do was lower her head slightly. Aurora licked and laved over the head of his cock and then paid attention to his frenulum. The groans emitting from his mouth let her know how much she was pleasing him. She hollowed her cheeks and sucked him into her depths, caressing the thick vein that ran down the underside of his erection. When she brought her mouth back up to the tip she suckled hard and saw how the muscles in his thighs quivered. Just as she was getting into a nice rhythm, Master Mike began to penetrate her pussy from behind. With the butt plug up her ass, a cock pushing into her pussy and another fucking her mouth, she was on an overload of sensation. Zings of pleasure battered her everywhere and she was in danger of climaxing. Inhaling deeply through her nose was enough to circumvent her rapacious arousal.

Her moan of pleasure was soon joined by Master Mac as she sucked him in, almost to the back of her throat. Once Master Mike was buried in her balls-deep, he held still, his hands gripping her hips firmly as he waited for her to adjust to his monstrous intrusion. Aurora withdrew her mouth from Master Mac's cock and gasped in air as her body adapted to his invasion. She was just thankful that Master Mac didn't force her to take him back into her mouth until she was ready.

"Okay, baby, are you ready?" Master Mike questioned.

"Yes, Master."

Master Mac didn't bother demanding verbally. He just ran the tip of his erection over the seam of her lips. Aurora didn't hesitate. She sucked him into the depths of her mouth, as far as she could without gagging. When she got back into a steady rhythm Master Mike began to move. He didn't start off slow and steady. No. He pounded into her from the get-go. She sobbed as pleasure assailed her from all sides, but not once did she stop giving Master Mac head. She could taste his spicy essence on her tongue, and with each bit of his cum that leaked into her mouth, she hungered for more. Aurora laved the underside of his cock with the flat of her tongue as she drew back until just the crown of his penis was in her mouth. Each time she enveloped him with her lips and mouth, she tried to take a little more.

She cried out as Master Mike's long, thick cock butted against her womb and liquid heat traveled throughout her blood. Just as she was about to go over the edge into nirvana, the bastard stopped.

"You don't get to come, sub," Master Mike panted. "This is punishment, remember?"

Aurora wanted to rail at him but didn't want the two Doms to have another reason to castigate her. She took Master Mac's cock into her mouth too far in a fit of pique and was about to gag when his voice soothed her anxiety.

"You can take me, honey. Breathe through your nose. There's a good girl," he crooned as he gripped her hair firmly, adding a bite of pain to her scalp which only seemed to raise her libido another notch. The fingers of his other hand stroked her throat as he coaxed her. "Swallow around me, Aurora. You can do it, sweetie."

She wanted to please him and found that if she breathed deeply and relaxed the muscles of her throat, she could indeed swallow around him without gagging or choking.

"Good girl, Aurora. God, her mouth is fucking heaven."

"So is her pussy. She's so damn tight, I'm not going to last," Master Mike said in a breathless, growly voice.

"You've got me there, honey. I want you to swallow everything I give you," Master Mac rasped.

Aurora felt Master Mac's cock expand as she twirled her tongue around the head of his dick, and then she slid back down over him as far as she could. When she swallowed around the head of his cock he gripped her hair tighter and held her still. He shouted just before he let loose. Load after load of cum spumed down her throat, and she swallowed rapidly, taking all he had to give. When she sucked the last of his essence up from his balls, he slowly eased his softening rod from her mouth.

"Lick me clean, honey," he gasped, and she pulled another groan from him as she did what he told her to. Finally he pulled his semi-flaccid penis from between her lips and stroked a hand over her hair, shoulders, and then down her restrained arms.

Aurora cried out when she felt Master Mike's latex-covered cock pulse inside her, and he groaned as he came. She had been so close and was hoping she would be able to come before he did even if it meant more punishment, but he froze inside her, and the jerking of his dick as he expended himself in her body wasn't enough to push her over the edge. Tears of frustration pricked the back of her eyes, but she refused to let them fall. All she'd dreamed about over the last twelve months was being loved by these two men, and even though it was happening she wasn't fulfilled in mind, body, or soul. She wanted more. Aurora wanted them to care for her as she cared for them. She didn't want to be just another sub for them to play with. She wanted to *mean* something to them.

She whimpered when Master Mike withdrew from her body and then hands released her from the spanking bench. Master Mac gently lifted her and carried her over to the swing, which was hanging from the ceiling by a large, sturdy hook and chain, as Master Mike went to clean up. She didn't protest when he placed her in the straps which supported her body, suspended by arms and legs, with another strap beneath her hips, face-up. She'd never used one of these swings before and felt a little insecure at first as she gripped the wide straps with her hands.

Master Mac must have seen her discomfit. "You are safe here, Aurora. We've tested this swing countless times. If it can hold our weight then it will definitely hold yours. Just relax, honey. We would never do anything to put you in danger."

"Where are we at, Aurora?" Master Mike asked as he came closer.

"Green, Master Mike."

"All right." Master Mike walked around to her head and lifted his hand. She inhaled deeply when she saw what he was holding. "Just remember to use 'yellow' if you're uncomfortable or uncertain about anything and 'red' if you want things to stop," he reiterated just before he placed the blindfold over her eyes.

Aurora's hearing seemed so much more enhanced without her eyesight. She heard every little rustle and movement the two men made, and her breath hitched in her throat as she contemplated what they were going to do to her. She didn't have to wait very long. Fingers caressed through her open, wet slit, and she couldn't prevent her body answering such an erotic pleasure. She bucked her hips up and sobbed but immediately froze when the digits withdrew.

"Don't move again, Aurora, or I'll spank that pretty little pussy until you're begging to be fucked," Master Mac said in a deep, rumbling voice.

She nibbled on her lower lip so she wouldn't tell him what she thought of that idea, but then she was gasping with pleasure as something cold, long, and thick was shoved into her pussy. The butt plug in her ass made her pussy so much tighter and her sheath rippled around the dildo or vibrator until it was pushed all the way inside her cunt. Aurora knew she was in deep trouble now. Masters Mike and Mac had already gotten off and now they were using toys on her. There was no way she could survive this punitive pleasure for long.

A whimper escaped as the toy was eased back out of her wet pussy. Then she sobbed as it was thrust in as far as it would go. After being taken to the edge of reason and back again, she wasn't sure how much longer she could survive without disgracing herself in the eyes of her two Doms by climaxing. The internal walls of her cunt rippled and heat filled her womb. Her pussy clenched and juices leaked from her vagina to run down and coat her anus. Just when she thought she was about to tip over into ecstasy the toy was pulled free from her pussy. She bit down on her lip so hard that she tasted blood. Aurora had never thought that she would have trouble controlling her pleasure when she had been so cold and unfeeling inside for so long, but these two Doms brought out the best of her, or maybe it was the worse.

Her two Masters were such kind men. She'd seen the way they took care of subs after playing with them at the club. Neither of them had ever said a bad word about anyone, and if someone needed help with anything they were always one of the first to volunteer. How could she not care for someone like that?

Aurora would love to be able to interact with people the way her two men did but she had been alone for so long, kept herself deliberately on the sidelines, she didn't know how to reach out. The yearning to do so was getting stronger and stronger and she didn't know how much longer she could stay closed up. Masters Mike and Mac had already worked away under her skin, but now they were a danger to her heart and she wasn't sure she liked that. These two men had gotten to her like no one else. She had been more open with them than any other person who had ever been in her life. Could she smash the ice around her heart and really let go with them? She wasn't sure, at least not yet.

Am I really such a coward?

She was so confused she could barely think straight. Her heart was pounding inside her chest at a rapid pace and she was breathing so fast she thought she may pass out from too much oxygen. Even though she couldn't see, pinpricks of light formed behind her closed eyelids and she started to feel light-headed. Her head lolled back on her shoulders and the deep cadence of two voices finally penetrated her lust-fogged mind.

"Shh, baby, take a deep breath and hold it for me," Master Mike said in a calm, low voice. She did what he said, and the light receded and the pounding of her rapid heartbeat finally began to slow. "Good girl, Aurora. That's it. Now exhale slowly." Again she obeyed his command. He talked her through her slightly panicked lust until finally her breathing slowed and the tightness she hadn't realized had invaded her muscles began to ease.

"Are you okay, honey?" Master Mac asked.

"Yes, Master Mac."

"Don't be afraid to use your safe word, Aurora."

"Yes, Master." Aurora sighed just before her lips were covered by Master Mac's. She almost felt like she was floating toward him, drowning in his clean, masculine scent and taste. When he finally lifted his mouth from hers, the simmering desire in her blood began to heat once more, but at least this time her muscles stayed relaxed and her body supine with none of the previous tension in sight.

Footsteps sounded down near her hips and she hoped whoever was between her legs wouldn't push her too hard or fast this time. She mewled when the dildo met her pussy and then slowly pushed in. With each forward thrust the speed was increased incrementally until it was being pumped in and out of her pussy at a rapid pace. Her internal muscles clenched and rippled, and before she could take her next breath she was on the cusp of climax once more. And once more the dildo was removed from her aching, needy pussy. Tears of frustration began to flow from her eyes and she was glad she had the blindfold on to hide her lack of control, but she should have known that she couldn't hide anything from the two men watching, teasing, and torturing her with mindless pleasure.

The blindfold was removed and it took her a few blinks to adjust her eyesight so it wasn't blurry, but when she saw Masters Mac and Mike watching her, she wished she'd kept them closed.

"Why are you crying, baby?" Master Mike asked, and Aurora was surprised by the warmth in his voice. Usually when he was in Dominant mode it was cool and his eyes ice cold, but now they were warm, almost as if he cared for her welfare.

"Why are you doing this to me? Why won't you let me come? Please, I don't think I can take much more," she cried.

"We'll let you come in a bit, Aurora, but first I want some answers."

Aurora couldn't stifle her sob of vexation from escaping, and she couldn't stem the flow of tears that were tracking over her cheeks. She should have known that these two men wouldn't give up until they had broken her wide open. A knot of pain and fear formed in her chest until she felt like she could barely swallow with her throat so tight.

"Why don't you ever talk about your family, baby?"

Of all the questions they could have asked, she hadn't seen that one coming. She bit her lip so hard one of her teeth pierced her flesh. She inhaled deeply and released it on a ragged sigh. Aurora could tell they weren't going to give her what she wanted until she had opened up with them. Tears pricked the back of her eyes, but she blinked them back and explained.

"My parents don't love me. They don't care about who I am or what I want. They only care about themselves and how their snobby friends perceive them."

She went on to explain how cold her parents were toward her and what had happened nearly two years ago to send her running and how she hadn't heard from them since. She felt as if she were floating outside herself when she explained about her family, and even she could hear the emotionlessness in her own voice.

"Jesus! I'm sorry they did that to you, baby." Master Mike stroked a finger down her cheek. "No parent should treat their child the way yours did or try to organize their lives for them. You're not unlovable, Aurora. Never doubt that. Your parents are the ones lacking. Not you."

Another layer of the ice coating her heart melted away at Master Mike's declaration. Was he true? Were her parents the ones who were damaged and not her after all?

"What do you feel toward us, Aurora?" Master Mac asked as he rubbed his thumbs over her face to wipe some of the moisture away. "Why is it that you only respond to us and no other Dom?"

The numbness which had prevailed as she explained about her family gave way to something much worse. Pain exploded in her chest and she felt like the walls encasing her heart had just shattered into a million pieces. Her mind was warring with her heart. She didn't want to answer those two questions and leave herself wide open, but since she was so het up with desire, pain, and yearning, beyond the point of reason, she heard her own voice echoing through the room as she yelled her answer.

"Because I love you!" she screamed and cried at the same time. "I love you both so much and no one else will do. You light up the room when you walk in. You're kind to everyone and would give someone the shirt off of your backs if you could. How could I not fall in love with you both?"

Chapter Ten

Mac felt guilty for pushing Aurora, but when she finally broke down he also felt relieved. He glanced at Mike and they quickly removed the ankle and wrist restraints from her limbs. He lifted her into his arms. She was sobbing her heart out, her body shaking as she cried out all her pain. He didn't try and speak meaningless platitudes as she cried. He carried her over to the sofa and sat down, cradling her in his arms and rocking her. When her tears didn't appear to be lessening, Mac became concerned that she was going to make herself sick. He gestured to Mike and then he followed his brother from the dungeon, down the hall, into the master bedroom where Aurora had spent the previous night, and then into the adjoining bathroom.

Mike turned the shower on to cool and Mac didn't even worry about his clothes getting wet. He stepped into the cubicle, stood under the lukewarm water, and sighed with relief when Aurora's crying began to slow until just the occasional hiccup erupted from her mouth. When she lifted her head, she drew in a shaky breath and exhaled slowly.

"I'm sorry."

"You have no need to be sorry, honey." Mac kissed her forehead and drew away again so he could see her eyes, but she ducked her head down until her brow rested on his shoulder. "Look at me, Aurora."

She lifted her head to meet his gaze once more.

"You have been carrying around so much emotional baggage for so long you were bound to break, honey. You needed to get rid of the pain and turmoil. Did you think we couldn't see how much you were hurting? We've asked you time and again over the last couple of days to open up with us, and you'd give a little bit of yourself, but for the most part, you kept yourself closed off from us.

"I love you, too, honey. I have for quite a while but we were just too dumb to do anything about it. I always saw the way you looked at us when we entered the club. You used to smile at everyone but us. God, how I wished you would turn that beautiful smile on us. You are such a caring, nurturing woman. Charlie took to you right away and so did Emma, from what Tank has said. You may have tried to keep your distance, but you have so much love to give, you just weren't able to manage to keep everyone at arm's length."

"You do? You really love me?" she asked on a gasp.

Mike stepped into the large shower. His brother had taken the time to strip out of his clothes and now he moved toward Aurora until she was sandwiched between the two of them.

Mike gently clasped her face between his hands and lifted it to his. He placed a gentle yet reverent kiss on Aurora's lips. "I love you very much, Aurora. If it hadn't been for me and my insecurities we would have been together so much sooner. I'm sorry I let one incident years ago affect our relationship. You are such a sexy, caring, passionate woman and anyone who says otherwise doesn't know you at all. You mean the world to me and I don't think I could breathe if you left."

"Are you sure? Please don't say that if you don't mean it."

"Look at me, baby. Really look at me," Mike demanded.

Mac heard Aurora's breath hitch in her throat when she looked at Mike. His brother had finally let go of his uncertainties and was letting her see how much she meant to him. She reached out and cupped Mike's cheek. "I love you, too." She reached out and hooked an arm around Mike's neck, drawing him closer, and then she kissed him long and deep. When she finally lifted her head they were both breathless.

Aurora looked up into Mac's eyes, and he let her see into his heart and soul. When he saw his feelings were reciprocated and that she did indeed love him and his brother, the slight knot of anxiety in his chest diminished. Mac bent down and ravaged her mouth. Now that she had opened up to them, the walls around her heart were down. He could see that she was no longer trying to protect herself from them and now that she had let them into her heart and soul they could begin the rest of their lives together. Mac knew they would have their ups and downs just like anybody else and it would take time for her to accept that their love was unconditional, but now they could make a start.

Mac slowed the kiss and then lowered her to her feet.

When she was steady, he and his brother began to take care of their woman. He began to wash her hair while Mike started to clean her body. By the time they were done the last of the tension which had invaded Aurora's body had dissipated. She stood leaning against the cool tile wall as if she was too tired to stand on her own.

After drying Aurora off, Mike picked her up and carried her to the bedroom. He placed her on the bed, and he and Mike got in on either side of her. Mac pulled her into his arms so that she was half lying on top of him. Mike spooned her from behind. She yawned a few times, and then he felt her body relax fully as she drifted into sleep.

"I think we finally got through to her," Mike whispered so he wouldn't disturb Aurora but loud enough so Mac could hear.

"Yeah, we did. Now all we have to do is get her to move in with us. I don't want her going home. I want her here with us all the time."

"As do I, but convincing Aurora is another thing."

"She can be really feisty when she has her mind made up." Mac shifted on his side and leaned his head on his hand as he stared down at their woman.

"Yeah, she sure can. Do you think she'll put up much of a fight?" Mike asked on a sigh.

"I don't know. We'll just have to wait and see."

Over the next hour the two men watched Aurora while she slept. Soon she was showing signs of awakening. She sighed and rolled in her sleep and then snuggled in closer to Mike. The hand she had resting on Mike's chest began to move as if she was caressing him. She made a cute little snuffling noise just before she blinked her eyes open. At first she looked confused but when she realized where she was her cheeks turned a delightful pink hue.

"Sorry, I didn't mean to fall asleep." She moved as if intending to sit up but Mike wrapped an arm around her waist and kept her where she was.

"You needed to rest, baby. You wore yourself out after crying so much."

"Um…" Aurora's cheeks turned even redder at the reminder of her small breakdown.

Mac threaded his fingers through her hair and then cupped her face. "Don't you dare be embarrassed, honey. You needed to get rid of all that pain inside. Now that you have we can move on with this relationship."

"We don't…"

Mike made a growling sound, cutting Aurora off before she completed her statement. He gave Mac a slight nod and he moved out of the way just in time. Mike moved quickly, shifting Aurora to her back, and then bracketed her with his body, covering hers without putting all of his weight on her, so he wouldn't crush her.

"Don't you dare deny what we have between us, baby. You love us and we love you. Nothing is going to change how we feel about each other. Now, I suggest you resign yourself to the fact that we are indeed in a relationship, because there is no way in fucking hell we are about to let you walk away from us."

Mac couldn't have said it better himself. Aurora turned her head slightly and met his gaze. There was still uncertainty in her eyes, but beneath that he could see hope and yearning. Their little sub wanted to be with them as much as they wanted to be with her, but she was still afraid.

Mike lifted his body up from hers and sat on his haunches between her legs. Mac moved in closer until his body was touching her side. "We want you to move in with us, honey. We want you in our lives and beds permanently."

"You barely know me," Aurora said with a quaver in her voice. "Why would you want me to live with you? What happens to me once the novelty of a new relationship wears off? What if one of you gets jealous? I couldn't bear the thought of coming between the two of you and causing a rift."

"That will never happen, Aurora," Mike said.

"We know you, honey." Mac drew her gaze back to his. "We have been watching you for nearly twelve months. You are such a kind, loving woman. We want the opportunity to get to know you better and for you to know us. There are still some issues we have to work on, and if you will give us time then we will learn more about each other as our relationship develops further. Underneath the cool, don't-touch-me façade is a heart of gold. Keep those walls down and we'll get to know each other inside out."

Mike threaded his fingers with hers. "We know there is no one else for you and it's the same for us. We may have frequented the club regularly, but if you had stopped to watch us when we played with the rare sub we have scened with, you'd realize that at no time have we had sex or touched them with real emotion. Most of the time we were at the club we were only there as monitors, and when we did play we only ever used toys or props such as floggers. The only time we have touched a sub was when we were placing and releasing the restraints or making sure they were comfortable."

Mac could see that Aurora was thinking back over the last months, and the frown which marred her face slowly changed to a stoic expression, and then her whole visage changed as she smiled.

"It's really true. You haven't fucked any of the other subs."

"No, baby, we haven't," Mike reiterated. "Now, if you give me your address and the keys to your place I'll get a couple of our employees to pack up all your stuff and put your furniture into storage. They will bring anything you want, your clothes, other personal effects, here to you."

"Back up the truck." Aurora frowned at Mike. "I haven't agreed to move in with you and there is no way I'm letting strangers go through my things. If I decide to move in here then I will pack my own things."

Mac's muscles were so tight he felt like he was going to explode, but he held his frustration in, because the last thing he wanted to do was send their little sub running. Even though he wanted to go all Dom on her over this issue, he decided pragmatism would win her over more.

"Will you at least think about moving in with us?"

"Okay, I can live with that," Aurora said.

"Thank God," Mac muttered as he breathed out, not having realized he'd been holding his breath until he spoke. The tension which had invaded his muscles also eased.

"Also, honey, we don't want you working reception tonight. We have no idea who has it in for Mike and me and now you. We don't want you getting hurt because of us." Mac clasped her hand after she propped herself up against the bedhead with pillows at her back.

"I appreciate your concern, but I'm going to work. I have an obligation to be there."

"I could call Turner and get someone else to cover for you." Mike was already flipping his cell phone open.

"Don't you dare!" Aurora glared at Mike. "I will be fine as long as I have one of the Doms by my side."

"I'll set it up with Turner," Mike conceded with a sigh of resignation. And then he spoke to Turner so that he and Mac would be on reception duty with Aurora until they knew she was safe. Mac was glad that he and Mike were the owners of their transport company since that allowed them much more leeway than being an employee. They would make sure that one of them was with their woman at all times. They didn't want her in the line of fire of whoever had it in for them. Until Detective Gary Wade was able to find out who the threats were coming from, their woman needed to be protected.

After finishing up with Turner, Mac lay down on the bed on his side and wrapped an arm around Aurora's hips. She gave a little squeak of surprise when he pulled her down until her body was flush with his, breast to chest. He stared deeply into her eyes and let her see how much he loved and wanted her. He watched as her lips parted and her breathing escalated, and he glanced down to the pulse beat in the base of her throat. Yep, she was getting aroused. His eyes wandered lower and he watched in fascination as her areolas began to pucker and her nipples began to harden.

Mac leaned in the last couple of inches until their lips touched. Her sexy little whimper of desire was enough to break his control. He opened his mouth over hers and devoured her, pushing his tongue into her moist cavern. He explored every inch of her recess and then caressed her tongue with his. She tasted so right and so sweet, he knew he would never get enough of her intoxicating flavor. When she pressed her breasts into his chest and then rolled her pelvis forward so that her mound rubbed against his stomach, he lost it.

He lifted his head just enough to pull his T-shirt off, and then he once more ravished her mouth while he undid his jeans and then pushed them down to his knees. Without breaking their kiss he shifted and eased Aurora onto her back while he kicked his jeans the rest of the way off. If it hadn't been for Mike pushing against his shoulder he would have been buried balls-deep in Aurora's wet pussy moments later.

"Condom," Mike growled loud enough to break through his passionate haze.

Mac slowed the kiss and then pushed himself up onto his knees where he sat gasping for breath between her shapely, sexy legs. He groaned when he saw her dilated pupils and kiss-swollen red lips. Mike slapped the condom packet against his chest, and without taking his eyes from her Mac ripped it open with his teeth, threw the packet to the side, and rolled the prophylactic down over his hard dick. Once done he smoothed his hands up Aurora's silky thighs until he came to her hip bones. He gripped her pelvis and rubbed his thumbs on the soft skin right next to her bones. She shivered, her skin trembled, and then goose bumps erupted all over her body.

"Looks like you just found a sweet spot, Mac," Mike said in a raspy voice and climbed onto the bed once more. Mac hadn't even been aware that Mike was stripping out of his own clothes since all of his attention had been on Aurora.

"I want to taste you, Aurora. I want to drink from your body," Mac panted.

"Oh, God."

"No, it's Mac, honey." He gave a chuckle and then scooted down the bed until he was lying on his stomach between her splayed limbs with his head hovering over her pussy.

Mac took a long lick of Aurora's pussy from her hole up to her clit. The little mewling sounds she made in the back of her throat let him know how much she liked what he did to her. He laved his tongue over her clit while he wrapped his arms around her thighs and spread them as far apart as she seemed comfortable with. He looked up her body when the next whimper she made was muffled and saw that Mike was kissing her rapaciously, while pinching and plucking at her nipples alternately with the fingers of one hand.

He took a deep breath and then he inserted a finger into her pussy hole. She bucked her hips up, silently begging for more, and he wasn't about to disappoint her. When he reached the webbing of his finger he pulled it out, and when he pressed back in it was with two fingers. She bucked and sobbed as he began to pump his digits in and out of her cunt, making sure to pass over her sweet spot with the pad of his fingers until she was writhing beneath him. His balls drew up close to his body and that warning tingle at the base of his spine let him know that he was on the verge of coming and he wasn't even inside her pussy yet. Her wet flesh quivered around his fingers as he pulled them free from her body.

Mike was now sucking on one of her nipples while squeezing the other one, and Aurora had her eyes closed with her head tilted back on the pillow. She had never looked sexier. He couldn't wait another minute. Gaining his knees again, he moved in close until the tip of his cock touched her wet pussy. Grasping the base, he rubbed it through her folds, coating the latex sheath with her natural lubrication, and then without any preamble he thrust into her until he was buried to the hilt.

She cried out and bucked up against him, but Mac wasn't about to let her take control. He grasped her hips firmly but not tight enough to hurt or mark her and then began to rock his hips. In and out he plunged until they were both moaning with bliss, but Mac wanted her so connected to him and Mike that leaving them wouldn't ever enter her mind. With a quick nudge of his elbow at Mike's arm, he nodded at his brother when Mike looked up at him and was thankful that he didn't need to verbalize what he wanted. Mike released her nipple from his mouth with a wet sucking sound and moved back so Mac could move.

He covered her body with his using his knees and elbows to brace his weight and slid his hands beneath the middle of her back. He rolled until he was lying on the bed with Aurora on top of him. Using his arms, he maneuvered her until her legs were straddling him with his cock still inside her, and then he spread his legs wide, opening her up for Mike.

Mike moved between their legs, and Mac heard the popping sound of a bottle of lube opening as his brother set about preparing their woman. Mac wrapped his arms around Aurora to keep her still, one hand high up between her shoulder blades and the other down low on her hips and the top of her ass.

"A little cold, baby," Mike said right before Aurora flinched.

"Oh," she mewled, and Mac figured Mike was caressing her ass.

"Fuck, her ass is so hot and tight," Mike gasped. "That's it, baby. Stay nice and relaxed for me. Two fingers now, Aurora."

"Shit, it burns," she panted.

"Do you want me to stop?" Mike asked.

"No. Please?"

"What do you want, honey?" Mac smoothed his hand over her hip.

"I need you both. God, I want you to both fuck me," she cried.

"Easy, baby, I need to prepare you so I don't hurt you." Mike looked up at him and Mac could see how on edge his brother was.

"Hurry the fuck up. I'm not gonna last much longer," Mac said in a growly voice.

"That's three fingers, baby. Just tell me to stop if it's too much. Okay?"

"Ooh," Aurora responded, and Mac took that for an affirmative.

"Take a deep breath for me, baby, and then let it out slowly," Mike ordered.

Aurora did as asked and then her pussy got a hell of a lot tighter. Mac shifted both hands down to her hips and withdrew his cock from her cunt until only half of him was inside her, giving Mike room so he could forge his way into her ass. With him in her pussy and Mike pushing into her ass, her muscles spasmed around his dick, making it hard for him to stay in control and not shoot his load. He began going through his time tables to hold his orgasm at bay.

"Oh my God. Oh my God," Aurora chanted.

"You okay, honey?" Mac gasped his question.

"Yes. Yes. Yes," she sobbed. "I need more."

Aurora planted her hands on Mac's chest and pushed up and back, causing Mike to curse when she cried out.

"I can't…I can't…I can't…"

Mac could see Aurora's whole body shaking and was about to call a halt to their lovemaking, but Mike questioned her before he could stop the proceedings.

"What can't you do, baby?"

"I can't get enough," she cried. "Fuck me, please. Take me fast, hard, and deep. I need you both. I love you both so much."

"Let's give our woman what she needs," Mac huffed and then shoved his dick back into her pussy hard and deep.

"Yes, more, more, more."

As Mac retreated, Mike advanced, and with each shove of their hips they increased the pace of their rocking until their flesh slapped against Aurora's. The cadence of their heavy breathing and bodies connecting was the only sound in the room as they fucked Aurora hard, fast, and deep. Mac looked up at Mike, saw the blissful, tortured expression on his brother's face, and knew he probably looked just like him. He threaded his fingers into Aurora's hair and tilted her face up for a kiss. Tears were streaming down her face and he cursed that he hadn't realized she was crying.

"Are we hurting you, honey? Why are you crying?"

"Shit." Mike stopped moving and tried to see her face.

"No! Don't stop. Please? You feel so good. I've never felt like this before. You make me feel so beautiful and loved and cherished. Make love to me please? I need to feel connected to you both."

Mac slammed his mouth down over hers and kissed her hungrily as he shoved his hips into hers. Their tongues dueled and parried in a dance mimicking the lower half of their bodies.

"God, your ass is heaven, baby. I can't hold off much longer. Push her over, Mac."

Mac slipped his hand down between their bodies until he reached the top of her slit. He lightly but rapidly caressed his finger back and forth over her clit. Her internal walls rippled and she pulled her mouth from his and gulped in air. Then she threw her head back and screamed. Her pussy gripped and let go, clasped, and released, bathing his cock, balls, and thighs in a gush of her juices as she climaxed. Aurora's whole body shook and convulsed as ecstasy washed over her.

The tingling at the base of his spine encompassed his whole lower body and sent fire shooting into his balls. His testicles drew up, and his seed was sucked from his body in a climax so intense he roared as his cum erupted from his dick into the end of the condom. Mike yelled as he, too, tipped over the edge and climaxed.

"Fuck, baby, that was so good, I don't think I can't stand." Mike kissed Aurora's shoulder.

Mac only just then realized that Aurora was a boneless heap on top of him. "Are you all right, honey?" When she didn't answer, he lifted his head and saw that her eyes were closed and her breathing was evening out. "She's asleep."

"Are you sure she's sleeping? Maybe she passed out. I swear I saw stars there for a moment." Mike slowly eased from her body and got off the bed. His brother walked with a wobbly gait as if he had been on a ship and didn't have his land legs back yet.

"I did, too. Can you fill the tub? We can bathe her, and after we're all cleaned up we can have lunch and head out."

"I was already on it," Mike replied and disappeared into the bathroom.

Mac turned and eased Aurora onto her side, and although his now-flaccid cock slipped from her body, he slid his arm beneath her head and hugged her close. His heart was full of love and contentment now that all he and Mike had to do was get their little sub to agree to move in with them.

Chapter Eleven

After a long day of working at the club, Aurora was exhausted. She rested her head on Mac's shoulder and closed her eyes just for a moment. When she became aware of the silence in the truck her eyelids fluttered open and she saw that they were home.

"Something's wrong," Mike said as he stared out the front windshield toward the front door of the house, and Aurora wondered why he hadn't parked the truck in the garage.

"Stay here, baby. Mac and I are going to check things out," Mike said as he opened the door to the truck. "Lock the doors after we get out."

Aurora shivered and frowned with confusion. She had no idea why they were wary but they knew their house better than she did. She squinted into the darkness, barely able to make out their shapes in the shadowy night. Movement off to the side caught her attention, and she watched as Mac skirted around the side of the house and then disappeared. She quickly looked back to see Mike enter the front door. No lights came on, which caused her anxiety to escalate. Just when she was about to unlock the doors and get out to investigate, a figure loomed at the passenger front door of the truck. She couldn't see who it was because it was so dark, but by the silhouette she knew it was a strange man.

She screamed as glass exploded toward her, cutting into her flesh. With trembling fingers she scrabbled with the seat belt catch and sobbed when it finally gave way, but she had been too slow. The passenger side door was opening and a hard hand gripped her ankle in an unforgiving grip. She kicked out with her other leg and felt a little satisfaction when the man cursed. Now that she could see his face because the interior light had come on when he had opened the door, she became more afraid. She'd never seen this person before but she could see the fury in his eyes. It was directed at her.

She tried to kick him again, but he was ready for her this time and caught her other ankle. His grip was bruising, and then he was pulling her across the bench seat toward him. Aurora yelled and struggled, hitting out, but she wasn't strong enough to escape his clutches. Stinging pain seared into the back of her thigh as she was pulled across the glass-covered seat, but she didn't have time to ascertain the damage done to her body. She needed to escape, and she wouldn't give up until she was free.

* * * *

Mike placed his hand on the doorknob, opened the front door, which wasn't locked, and reached for the light switch. He cursed under his breath when nothing happened. The power must have been cut, which also meant that the security system was down. He wondered why his cell phone hadn't alerted him to the situation. He hoped that Derrick and Garth were aware of what was going on and were on their way over or had called the cops. He reached into his pocket and pulled out his cell phone and called Gary. When the other man answered he didn't give him time to speak.

"We've been broken into, the power has been cut, and Mac and I are checking things out. I'd appreciate it if you could get your ass over here as quickly as possible." Mike had whispered the whole conversation, hoping that whoever had broken in couldn't hear him or see the light from his digital display. Once he finished talking he disconnected the call and waited until his eyes adjusted to the lack of light. He carefully moved along the hall, staying close so he wouldn't be an easy target. His heart beat rapidly as adrenaline spiked through his system, and he was glad for the hormone which would benefit him if he came face-to-face with the intruder.

Mike stopped near the kitchen door and peered around the corner. He couldn't see much, but from what he could make out there was nothing out of the ordinary in the room. He headed toward the bedrooms, being careful not to make a noise. Just as he passed the bathroom he felt the air near his head move. He spun around but he wasn't fast enough. Pain exploded in his head, and his knees buckled. Mike fought nausea which threatened to erupt, but he breathed deeply and waited for the throbbing in his head to lessen. He tried to see where his assailant was but it was still too dark. Moving slowly, he got to his hands and knees and sighed with relief when he realized whoever had attacked him was gone. Slowly he pushed up and then got to his feet and leaned against the wall to regain his equilibrium when nausea once more threatened. Just as he pushed off the wall he heard a scream and began to run.

* * * *

Mac ducked around the side of the house and saw that the side door access to the garage stood wide open. Being careful not to make a sound, he entered, but there was no one in sight. A noise toward the back of the house drew him out into the night toward the garden shed at the rear of the property. The tin door was ajar and light was emanating from within. He edged his way nearer and then peeked around the side of the door. No one was inside, but sitting in the middle of the shelf on the far side was a large flashlight. Since none of the lights inside had come on, he decided that the light would come in handy and hurried across to retrieve it. Just as he placed his hand on the handle, the door to the shed slammed closed and the bolt slid across, locking him inside.

Fuck! Now what am I going to do? Shit, Aurora. I need to get to Aurora.

Mac swung the flashlight around, looking for something to use to help him escape. His eyes alighted on the garden shears and he prayed they would be enough. Setting the light on the floor, he got down on his hands and knees and began to work.

* * * *

Aurora cried out when her shoulders hit the step of the truck as she was dragged from the seat. Her breath left her lungs in an *oomph* when her back landed on the hard concrete driveway. Pain radiated out from everywhere, but what sent her into a panic was the fact that she couldn't breathe. It felt like hours but she knew it was probably only seconds before she was able to draw any air into her oxygen-starved organs.

Once she became aware of her surroundings, she began to fight anew. The man was pulling her to her feet and then trying to drag her away. She dug in her heels and used all of her body weight to prevent him from taking her, but she was too small to slow him down.

She tried to trip him and then kick him but nothing seemed to work. When she dug her nails into his arm with her free hand he cursed and then charged at her. Her world spun and then she was over his shoulders, her body lying across them behind his neck, and he was heading toward a car parked a little down the road. Aurora knew if she didn't escape now that her life would be in danger. She renewed her struggles, kicking and bucking, hoping the asshole would drop her. A hard slap landed on her face, causing her to cry out. Just when she thought she was going to lose the fight she noticed headlights coming toward them.

Using every bit of strength she could, Aurora wrapped her hands around the fucker's neck and squeezed. He growled and slapped her again, but she wasn't about to give in. She dug her nails into the skin of his neck and dragged them along his flesh. He yelped and then she was falling. Her body slammed into the road, her head bouncing off the black tarmac, and she saw stars. She couldn't see where he was but used her legs to kick and flailed her arms, hoping to keep him at bay.

A familiar voice finally penetrated her pain-induced fog.

"Put your hands in the air. *Now*," Detective Gary Wade snapped out.

Aurora's vision finally cleared and she looked up to see the bastard crouching over her with a gun pointed at her head. As she stared down the barrel of the gun, she began to shiver with fear and cold. She'd never felt so cold in her life. A trickle of warmth dripped down her leg and she wondered how badly she was cut.

What an odd thing to think about when I'm about to die.

The man grabbed hold of her hair and tugged her to her feet. Her legs were shaking so much she could barely stand. If it wasn't for the fucker holding her up she would still be in a heap on the ground.

"Drop your weapon and let the woman go," Gary ordered.

"Do you think I'm fucking stupid? As soon as I release her you'll shoot me."

"Not if you drop the gun. Let her go and drop the gun at the same time."

Aurora didn't know how much longer she could stay upright. She felt weak and was sure it was from loss of blood as well as shock. Her teeth chattered, and even though she was aware of everything going on around her, everything seemed surreal. As if she was living a dream.

* * * *

Mike could see a dark trail on the concrete driveway and knew it was Aurora's blood. He followed the trail of blood and prayed the whole time that she was alive. When he reached the road, the trail merged with the blacktop of the bitumen, but he didn't need to see it anymore. He hurried as much as he could, his head pounding with every step he took. Headlights in the distance illuminated the road and he saw that the man was carrying Aurora across the top of his shoulders toward a car about a hundred yards ahead. She was fighting him with everything she had. When he was fifty yards away he moved off to the side of the road onto the grass shoulder so his footsteps were muffled.

The car came to a screeching halt and he nearly sagged with relief when he heard Gary ordering the man to let Aurora go. The bastard had flung her from his shoulders and he felt sick when she landed on the road with a dull thud, and now he was crouched over her. As Mike moved closer to Aurora and the asshole, he spotted Mac across the yard, also making his way toward them. They communicated silently, using tactics they learned in the military, and planned their next move.

He was only twenty yards away when the asshole lifted Aurora by her hair and held the gun to her head. There was no way in hell he was letting the love of his life die, when they had only just found each other.

Mike crept along and when he was closer moved back onto the road. Stones crunched beneath his feet and the bastard turned and pointed the gun in his direction. Mike went flying through the air and hit the ground hard, as he dove out of the line of fire.

He lifted his head when he heard the scuffle and winced when Mac took a punch to the jaw. While he had distracted Aurora's assailant and drawn his gunfire, Mac had been moving toward him from behind. The gun went flying and then Mac's fist hit the bastard in the face over and over again. Finally his brother stopped punching and he waited with bated breath hoping the fucker was down for the count. Mac was still straddling him with a raised fist, but when the prick didn't move he slowly rose to his feet. Gary rushed forward, rolled the attacker onto his stomach, pulled his arms behind his back, and cuffed him.

Mike scrambled to his feet and rushed over to Aurora, who was lying in the middle of the road motionless.

"Aurora, baby, where are you hurt?" Mike asked.

"Speak to us, honey," Mac demanded as rushed over to their woman.

She smiled up at him and Mac and then her smile turned to a frown. Her eyes slid closed. Mike and Mac both went to their knees trying to see where she was injured. Mac shone the flashlight he held in his hand over her body. Her cheek was red where the asshole had struck her, but other than that Mike couldn't see any other damage.

"Help me roll her over, Mike." Mac placed the light on the ground. "We need to check her for injuries."

Mike pulled his T-shirt off, wadded it up, and placed it under Aurora's head. With care they turned her onto her side. Mac snatched up the light and moved it up and down her body. Her left thigh had a long jagged cut on the back, and both her legs were covered in blood.

"Jesus," Gary gasped when he saw Aurora's wound. "Paramedics are on the way. I should have killed that bastard but I didn't want to shoot in case I hit Aurora."

Mac stripped off his T-shirt and put it over the cut on Aurora's leg and applied pressure. More police cars and two ambulances arrived on the scene. The paramedics assessed Aurora and then loaded her up on a stretcher. Mike followed them to the ambulance and was about to get in when Gary's voice stopped him.

"Do either of you know who this asshole is?" Gary shone a light on the face of the man currently being wheeled to the other ambulance.

"Shit. Yeah, it's Billy Smith. He owns another moving company here in town."

"Thanks, I'll be by the hospital as soon as I've finished up here to get your statements."

Mike nodded and then got into the ambulance.

"I'll get the truck and follow," Mac called out and then ran back toward the house.

One paramedic attended to Aurora while the other saw to the cut on his head. Mike reached over and clasped Aurora's hand, praying that she would be all right.

Chapter Twelve

Aurora woke to the sound of beeping and knew she was in a hospital. The blood pressure cuff around her upper arm whirred quietly as it pumped up and squeezed, and then as it released it beeped out some sort of message or alert unknown to her. She licked her lips, trying to moisten them, but even her tongue felt dry so it didn't make any difference. She finally became aware that both her hands were being held and struggled to pry her eyelids open, having to blink a few times to dispel the haze in front of her. Turning her head to the side, she met aqua-blue eyes.

"How do you feel, honey?" Mac asked.

"Like I've been pulled through a hedge backward," she answered in a husky voice.

Mac released her hand and reached for the jug of water on the table near the foot of the bed. He poured water into a cup, stuck a straw into it, and then moved the couple of steps nearer to her head. She sipped gratefully and thanked him after quenching her thirst. She looked to the other side of the bed and saw Mike sleeping with his head on the bed close to her hip. There was a small bandage just above his left temple.

"Is Mike all right?" she asked in a whisper so she wouldn't wake him.

"He'll be fine, honey. He's got a couple of stitches where that asshole clouted him with a bat and a headache, but other than that he's as right as rain."

"Thank God," she said and gently stroked her fingers through Mike's hair, making sure to stay well away from his injury.

"You, however, are another story," Mac said with a frown.

"I'm fine, Mac. A little achy and my muscles are stiff, but I'm alive."

"And thank God for that," Mike rasped as he sat up. "I have never been so scared in my life, baby. I thought you were dying."

"It takes more than being dropped on the ground to kill me." Aurora laced her fingers with Mike's once more.

"You are going to have to take it easy for quite a while, honey. The doctor stitched up your leg, but you lost a lot of blood and they had to give you two pints. You will be really tired for a while and you won't be going back to work for at least three weeks," Mac stated in a firm voice.

"Three weeks! Shit. Well, then I guess I had better move in with you so you can both take care of me."

"What?"

"Do you mean that, baby?" Mike asked.

"Yes. When that asshole was trying to kidnap me I vowed that if I survived then I would move in with you as soon as I could. I love you both, so much, and don't want to waste another minute. I want to be with you. I need to be with you. I want to spend the rest of my life with you both by my side."

"God, honey, you've made me so happy," Mac said in a husky voice. He lifted her hand and kissed the back of it.

"I love you so much, Aurora. I want to wake up with you every morning. I want to spend each spare minute holding you, loving you and maybe one day, watch your belly grow big with our child."

"Are you ..."

"Shh, baby, just rest. I don't want you to tire yourself out," Mike said.

"Ah, glad to see you're awake, young lady," the elderly doctor said as he entered the room. "You listen to your young man. It would be best to rest and recuperate for as long as you can. If you push yourself too hard, you might just end up back in here, and I'm sure you don't want that."

"No, sir," she replied but lowered her eyes so her men couldn't see the gleam of determination she was sure she couldn't hide.

"Good. Now the nurse will be in shortly with your release forms. You will need to see your regular GP to get the stitches removed from that leg, and of course I already have a detailed report for you to hand over to your doctor. You have no concussion, and other than a swollen bruised cheek and bruising to your back, you are otherwise healthy. Do you have any questions?"

"No. Thank you, Doctor."

"You're welcome. When you get home make sure you go straight to bed, and take him with you." The doctor pointed toward Mike. "He has a slight concussion but refused to leave your side. Stubborn young man."

"You don't know the half of it," Aurora muttered, and to her chagrin the doctor heard her. He threw back his head and roared with laughter, and then he surprised the crap out of her.

"We Doms tend to be a stubborn lot." He winked at Aurora and then left the room still chuckling.

"Close your mouth, honey," Mac said, gently squeezing her hand.

She snapped her mouth closed with an audible click.

"Do one of you want to tell me who that man was?"

"He was the doctor who treated you, baby."

"No, not the doctor. I meant the one who tried to abduct me."

Mac cleared his throat. "He was Billy Smith, owner of Smith Movers. Apparently his business started going down the tubes when we started our own company, and instead of looking into ways of fixing things he just went to the bank and borrowed more and more money. Over the years our company grew and he became angry at our success. He finally closed the doors and ceded bankruptcy last week. Rather than looking at his business acumen, he became jealous of our success and blamed us for his problems. Smith snapped and came after us, by breaking and entering into our home and warehouse. When that didn't work he decided to hurt us where it would hurt most and came after you.

"He'd been watching us for a while, and when you entered our lives he decided you were the better option to hurt us."

Aurora shivered. Mike rubbed his thumb over the back of her hand. "He can't hurt you anymore, baby. Gary had to shoot him in the shoulder when the asshole tried to escape when he pulled him from his patrol car and was trying to get him into the precinct. He's currently recovering, but he has a guard twenty-four seven. When he's well enough he will be incarcerated until he's up for a trial hearing."

"Will I have to testify?" she asked.

"I'm not sure. We can ask Gary when he comes to take your statement. He's already been in to take ours, but since he was on the scene he doesn't think so. Gary hopes that your statement will be enough. But don't worry, baby. If you do you won't have to do it alone."

Aurora sagged with relief and then looked up as the nurse entered the room. An hour later they were on the way home.

* * * *

Over the next two weeks visitors from the club dropped in regularly. Masters Turner and Barry along with Charlie brought over a casserole and stayed for a chat and then left again. Masters Gary, Tank, and Jack also popped in a few times, and her Doms took advantage of Master Jack's doctoring skills to give her a checkup. He also removed the stitches from the back of her thigh when they were due to come out.

Aurora had been thankful that the doctor at the hospital had advised her to rest up because those first two weeks she was very lethargic and would find herself drifting off to sleep at the blink of an eye. But now that she was into her third week of recuperation she was beginning to feel like her old self again.

Mac and Mike had hardly left the house. They both worked from their home office, keeping up with the day-to-day running of their business, and even though she appreciated their thoughtfulness and care she was beginning to get cabin fever. She wanted to be back at work but she also craved her men to make love with her. Although she had spent each and every night sleeping between her two men, neither of them had made a move toward her and she was becoming antsy.

With a sigh she clicked off the TV and pushed up from the sofa to her feet. She decided a soak in the tub might help relax her and relieve some of her frustration. Then a plan began to form, and she smiled to herself as she headed down the hall toward their bedroom and the en suite bathroom. She filled the large spa bath, added some soaking salts to the water, and stripped out of her clothes. Giving a sigh as the warm water enveloped her, she then picked up the sponge, poured some bath gel onto it, and began to wash. After washing every inch of her body she brought the sponge back down between her legs and moaned as the slight abrasion caressed her clit. With her spare hand she reached up and pinched first one nipple and then the other. The faster she moved the sponge over her pussy, the louder she moaned.

Aurora had her eyelashes lowered but kept a surreptitious eye on the open bathroom door. She had expected her men to rush in after the first groan, but still they hadn't made an appearance. *Maybe I'm not being loud enough.*

Aurora pressed the sponge harder against her clit and rubbed faster. Her moans and groans escalated, and she closed her eyes as pleasure assailed her. She was right on the verge of climax. A couple more strokes and she would fly over the edge.

She yelped when a warm, masculine hand plucked the sponge from her hand and threw it aside. In the next instant she was being lifted out of the bath and was standing on the mat.

"You are in big trouble, sub." Master Mike pinned her with his ice-cold blue eyes.

Oh goody. Aurora mentally cheered.

"Are you allowed to pleasure yourself, honey?" Master Mac narrowed his eyes at her, his face a cool mask of indifference.

Aurora looked from one Dom to the other. If she didn't love them and didn't know them, she would have been shaking in her boots, but she could see their love for her shining out from their gazes and let them see how much she loved them in return.

Smack.

"Yow." Aurora went to rub her stinging backside.

"You don't have permission to move, sub, and we're still waiting for your answer."

"No, Master Mac."

"I think our sub needs to be punished. Maybe a reminder of what discipline feels like will get her back in hand," Master Mac said as he finished drying her off.

"I agree." Master Mike scooped her off her feet, cradled her in his arms against his chest, and carried her into the bedroom.

Her eyes alighted on the bed, and her heartbeat raced when she saw the cuffs already secured to the rings on the bed. He placed her in the middle of the mattress, and her two Doms restrained her quickly. She was lying on her back, her arms above her head and her legs spread wide. Once she was tethered, Master Mac began to strip. He practically tore his clothes from his body, and then he was crawling onto the bed between her legs.

Master Mike hurriedly removed his clothes and got on the mattress beside her. As he leaned down and took her mouth, Master Mac lowered his head and began to lap at her pussy.

Aurora moaned and arched her hips into Master Mac's mouth and then groaned with frustration when he lifted his head. Master Mike kissed and licked his way down her cheek, the line of her jaw, down her neck, heading toward her chest.

"If you move again, little sub, I'll flip you over and paddle your ass. Do you understand?" Master Mac asked.

"Yes, Master Mac."

"Hmm, see that you obey me, honey, or I'll bring you close to orgasm over and over without letting you come."

Aurora knew that he wouldn't hesitate to do what he said, so she held still. It was one of the hardest things she'd ever had to do, fighting her body's instincts. Master Mac licked over her clit and sucked the little pearl into his mouth. She whimpered as pleasure assailed her, fanning the embers of her arousal into white-hot flames. Master Mike suckled at one nipple firmly, and then he crushed it against the roof of his mouth with his tongue while pinching the other between thumb and finger.

She cried out at the painful pleasure, and cream leaked from her pussy. She was so hot and turned on she was in danger of climaxing before one of her men even entered her body. Panting helped a little but not enough. Master Mac pushed a finger inside her cunt and began to pump it in and out. He must have felt how close she was to orgasm because a moment later he withdrew.

"Please, Masters?"

"Please what, sub?" Master Mike asked.

"Please love me, Masters."

"We already do, honey. God, I love you so much," Master Mac declared just before he sank his cock into her balls-deep. "Oh yeah. You feel so fucking good, Aurora."

"I love you, baby," Master Mike said as he tapped his hard cock lightly against her cheek.

She didn't need to be asked. Aurora opened her mouth wide and sucked him in. She bobbed up and down, swirling, twirling, and laving her tongue over every inch of his hot, smooth velvet skin. Master Mac began to thrust his hips, stroking his dick in and out of her wet pussy. She moaned around the cock pressing in and out of her mouth, which caused Master Mike to growl with pleasure. So she did it again and again and took him to the back of her throat and swallowed around the broad, bulbous tip.

"Fuck!" Master Mike roared, and then he was shooting his load onto her tongue and down the back of her throat. When he'd finished releasing into her mouth he began to pull out, and she sucked him clean, right before he collapsed on the bed beside her.

Master Mac slid a hand beneath her ass and kneaded a cheek right before his finger was pushing against her rosette as his hard rod slid in and out of her pussy. Her blood heated until she felt as if she was melting. Her womb became heavy and her internal walls rippled as more juices leaked from her cunt. And then his finger penetrated her ass, which was enough to tip her over the edge. Aurora screamed as rapture washed over her. Her pussy contracted and twitched over and over, and she cried out at such intense pleasure. Just as the climax began to wane, Master Mac removed his hand from her bottom and slipped it in between their bodies.

Her breath hitched in her throat and she opened her mouth on a silent scream as she once more reached orgasm. Master Mac's cock twitched inside her, adding to her pleasure, and then he yelled as he, too, reached his release. Even though he was wearing a condom, she still felt the warmth of his seed as it was captured in the tip of the latex.

Aurora's arms dropped from around Master Mac's neck to the bed and she lay gasping for breath in a boneless heap.

Chapter Thirteen

Aurora knew something was up with her two men, but even though she asked, they just smiled and diverted her attention. It had been six months since she had moved in with them and she couldn't have been happier. They lavished her with love and attention and she felt like she truly belonged for the first time in her life. She was home and deliriously content with her Doms.

She looked up when the door to the club opened and greeted Masters Gary, Tank, Jack, and their sub, Emma. Emma gave her a knowing look and smiled as she gave her a wink.

Now what's that all about?

The quartet disappeared through the internal club doors, and Aurora sighed. She didn't want to be manning the desk tonight. She wanted to be with her men who were currently on monitor duty.

The doors to the great room burst open, and Masters Garth and Derrick came around behind the desk with a new sub in tow.

"Aurora, we are going to take over for a while and show Krista the ropes. Your Masters want you inside."

"Okay. Thank you, Master Derrick." She hurried across the foyer and into the great room. Aurora spied her Doms standing at the bar drinking water and talking to Masters Barry and Turner. When she got to their sides, she waited patiently with her head lowered and her hands clasped behind her back.

"Give me your wrists, sub," Master Mac commanded.

Aurora lifted her hands and Master Mac placed the cuffs around her wrists and then ran a finger under the edge, making sure they weren't too tight.

"Such a good little sub," Master Mike praised, and then he clicked the cuffs together in front of her.

Master Mac grasped the small chain between her restrained hands and led her toward the stage off to the side of the dance floor. She followed him up the steps, and her respiration increased as she wondered what her two men were about to do.

Master Mike came up behind her and moved her until she was standing beneath the chain dangling from the ceiling, but instead of raising her hands above her head and securing her to the chain, he moved her until she was facing toward the dance floor and bar and then unhooked her cuffs.

The chatter slowly diminished when the music was turned off, and she waited with trepidation as her two Doms stared down at her. Both her Masters went down on one knee and then each took hold of one hand.

"Aurora, you have given me such joy and mean more to me than words could ever say. Will you do us the honor of marrying us?" Master Mike asked.

Tears filled her eyes and spilled down her cheeks. She was so full of love and emotion she couldn't speak. She clutched at their hands and nodded.

"I can't hear you, sub," Master Mike said in a raspy voice.

"Yes. Yes, I will marry you both. God, I love you both so much."

Masters Mac and Mike gained their feet, and Master Mike slipped a ring onto her left hand. She looked down at her finger, and even though her vision was blurry from her tears the ring sparkled in the muted light. A large diamond graced her finger, and on either side were two smaller sapphires set in yellow gold.

Master Mike kissed her long and hard, and when he released her Master Mac took his place. When he weaned his mouth from hers she became aware of the whistles, cheers, and clapping from club members and patrons. Master Mac moved around behind her, and something cool touched the skin of her throat.

"This collar matches your ring, honey, and lets all the single Doms know you are taken."

She touched the cool metal with her fingertips and felt the three gems set into the choker band. Master Mac lifted her up and carried her through the cheering throng and headed toward the exit with Master Mike rushing ahead to open the doors.

Aurora nuzzled her nose into his neck and breathed in his wonderful masculine scent.

Masters Garth and Derrick and Krista called out their congratulations as she was carried out the large wooden double doors.

Aurora was looking forward to the years to come with her two men. She looked back over how lonely and despondent she had been when she thought her two men hadn't realized she existed. It was amazing how things turned out for the best in the long run.

She had never imagined that she would end up with two Doms of her very own.

THE END

WWW.BECCAVAN-EROTICROMANCE.COM

ABOUT THE AUTHOR

My name is Becca Van. I live in Australia with my wonderful hubby of many years, as well as my two children.

I read my first romance, which I found in the school library, at the age of thirteen and haven't stopped reading them since. It is so wonderful to know that love is still alive and strong when there seems to be so much conflict in the world.

I dreamed of writing my own book one day but, unfortunately, didn't follow my dream for many years. But once I started I knew writing was what I wanted to continue doing.

I love to escape from the world and curl up with a good romance, to see how the characters unfold and conflict is dealt with. I have read many books and love all facets of the romance genre, from historical to erotic romance. I am a sucker for a happy ending.

For all titles by Becca Van, please visit
www.bookstrand.com/becca-van

Siren Publishing, Inc.
www.SirenPublishing.com

CPSIA information can be obtained at www.ICGtesting.com
Printed in the USA
LVOW10s2057030415

433208LV00022B/519/P